DR. QUINN
Medicine Woman
NEW FRIENDS

NEW FRIENDS

An original novel by Colleen O'Shaughnessy McKenna
Based on characters from *Dr. Quinn, Medicine Woman*

SCHOLASTIC INC.
New York Toronto London Auckland Sydney

Photo credits: Cover, Peter Kredenser. Insert, page 1 (top and bottom): Peter Kredenser; page 2 (top): Cliff Lipson, (bottom): Peter Kredenser; page 3 (top and bottom): Peter Kredenser; page 4 (top): Peter Kredenser, (bottom): Cliff Lipson; page 5 (top): Peter Kredenser, (bottom): © 1995 Peter Kredenser; page 6 (top and bottom): © 1995 Peter Kredenser; page 7 (top): Peter Kredenser, (bottom): Charles Bush; page 8 (top): © 1995 Peter Kredenser, (bottom): Peter Kredenser.

ISBN 0-590-60372-8

12 11 10 9 8 7 6 5 4 3 2 1   5 6 7 8 9/9 0/0

Printed in the U.S.A.   40

First Scholastic printing, November 1995

Dedicated with much love to my daughter,
Collette, in celebration of her
twenty-first birthday.

— C.O.M.

DR. QUINN
Medicine Woman
NEW FRIENDS

1

The sun's rays painted the wooden floorboards as the chilly Colorado wind rattled the windowpanes. Colleen Cooper flipped onto her stomach and snuggled deeper into the soft quilt. She smiled, remembering the long peaceful hours spent stitching the quilt with Dr. Mike, her new mother.

"Rise and shine!" Dr. Mike called from downstairs.

Colleen sat up in bed, yawning as she leaned over to lift the white curtain. The Colorado Rockies were always in sight, yet still so far away. One day she would climb to the highest peak, close her eyes, and stretch both arms up toward heaven. Maybe then Colleen would feel closer to her real mother, Charlotte. How could such a strong woman have died from the bite of such a small snake?

"Hey, sleepyhead, wake up!" Dr. Mike stuck

her head inside the room. "You don't want the spelling bee to start without you."

Colleen scrambled out from under the quilt. "I'll be out in a second, Ma."

Dr. Michaela Quinn grinned. "Take a whole *minute*, Colleen. I'm sure Reverend Johnson doesn't want you showing up at school in your nightgown."

Colleen hurried to the nightstand and splashed cold water on her face. She was anxious to get to school and start the spelling bee. The Reverend had said the top two finalists would travel to Weisport to compete in the tri-town spelling bee. In another year or two, when the north–south railroad had laid track to Denver all the way from the Rio Grande, there would be three or four dozen schools competing. Maybe the next spelling bee would be in Denver!

Colleen slid her school dress over her head, hoping her best friend, Becky, had remembered to study her word list last night. It would be perfect if the two of them were chosen to take the stage to Weisport.

"I can't wait for some biscuits, Colleen," Matthew called out. He was five years older than Colleen and lived in Dr. Mike's old cabin. But when he worked at the new house, he ate breakfast there.

"Morning," Colleen said as she hurried into the

kitchen. She ran her fingers through her thick blond hair and hurried to get her breakfast. She smiled at her brothers. "Brian, did you study your words for the spelling bee?"

Brian took a gulp of milk. "No." He glanced up quickly at Dr. Mike. "I mean, I did, sorta, kinda a little bit." Brian leaned over and tugged on Colleen's sleeve. "But I bet Laura McCoy was up all night studying her words. Laura told Missy and Paul that you are the dumbest girl in the whole school. Says the only reason you get A's is 'cause the Reverend used to be sweet on Ma, and since he's the new teacher . . ."

"Brian Cooper!" said Dr. Mike. "The Reverend and I were never really *sweet* on each other. Don't go carrying tales."

"That was before Dr. Mike and Sully got married anyway," added Matthew. "Carrying tales will get you in trouble, little brother."

Brian ducked his head. "I only carried them here. Laura said if Colleen is picked to go to Weisport and she ain't, it's because she lives atop the saloon while Colleen gets to live out here."

"That's the biggest lie I've ever heard." Colleen pushed the freshly made eggs away. Laura McCoy had just swiped her appetite.

"Of course you and Colleen live out here with me and Sully. We're a family now," said Dr. Mike. "We live together."

"I'd like to live atop the saloon," Brian said. "Petey says you can hear the piano playing all night."

"Laura has no call to tell lies about me," insisted Colleen. "Maybe she doesn't know that I grew up in a boardinghouse just down the street from the saloon." Colleen stood up and started to pace. "Ohhhh, who does that Laura McCoy think she is, anyway? She never set eyes on me before school started."

"I was gonna punch Petey McCoy in the nose, but I knew I'd get in trouble," mumbled Brian.

"Wise choice, Brian," laughed Matthew.

Dr. Mike pushed her chair away from the kitchen table. "Time for school. Matthew, Sully wants to talk to you about repairing the east fence today. He's been out there since the chickens were up."

Brian stood up, wiping his mouth on his sleeve. "I *did* tell Petey that Colleen has lots of chores to do. I told him she helps you at the clinic, too, Ma." Brian grabbed his lunch sack and headed out the door. "Told Petey McCoy that Colleen Cooper sure ain't no princess."

"She *isn't* a princess," corrected Dr. Mike.

"Yeah, that's what I told him." Brian shouted from the yard. "Hurry up, Colleen. Bye, Matthew. Bye, Ma."

Colleen grabbed her sack and an apple from the bowl. "I don't understand people some days. Dr.

4

Mike, why would Laura say that about me? I'm always nice to her, even when she's rude."

"Ignore her," suggested Matthew. "Might be hard in a one-room schoolhouse, but you can try."

Dr. Mike refilled Matthew's coffee cup. "Laura must be unhappy. She's new, Colleen. Give her a little bit of time. Remember how unfriendly most folks were to me when they found out I was the new town doctor?"

Colleen laughed. "Well, they were expecting a man. Nobody out here ever saw a female doctor. I guess the townsfolk didn't give you a very warm welcome."

Dr. Mike reached out and hugged Colleen. "Your mother did. You, Matthew, and Brian helped me settle into my first house."

Colleen was silent with the knowledge that when she first set foot in that abandoned cabin, her mother had been alive. The second time was to carry in her personal belongings and stay.

"I better get going," said Matthew. "See you for supper."

Colleen reached for her schoolbooks and followed Matthew out the door. "Dr. Mike, have I changed since Ma died? Do you think Laura McCoy is seeing something in me that's mean?"

"Not a bit."

Colleen smiled. "Thanks. Wish me good luck with the spelling bee."

"Good luck, Colleen. And remember, Laura is

the new girl in town now. Maybe *she* needs a friend."

As Colleen hurried down the road to catch up with Brian, she realized Dr. Mike was right. Laura McCoy didn't seem to have any friends in town. Guess nobody ever told her it was easier to attract bees with honey instead of with vinegar.

"I guess giving Laura another chance won't kill me," Colleen decided. Besides, with the spelling bee, the day was going to be filled with so much excitement, Colleen didn't have a speck of room in her heart for anything but happiness. Once Reverend Johnson announced that Colleen and Becky would represent Colorado Springs in the state championship, they would be too busy packing to think about anything except the fun they would have in Weisport.

2

"Hey, wait for me, Brian!" Colleen hurried to catch up.

Brian stood in the middle of the dirt road, shielding his eyes against the sun. "Colleen, what will you do if Reverend Johnson asks you a word so long you can't figure a way to spell it?" Brian swung his schoolbooks to his other shoulder. "Can you ask him for another word?"

Colleen shook her head and grinned. "No. I'll sound it out real carefully and then try hard to spell it." Colleen gently elbowed her little brother. "Dr. Mike reads to you all the time, Brian. I bet you know a lot of words. The spelling bee is going to be so much fun."

"I'd rather go fishin'."

Colleen stopped, craning her neck. "Who's that charging up the hill, Brian? It's Becky!"

Brian squinted. "Yeah. She sure is running. Wonder who's chasing her?" Brian laughed. "Hey,

Becky. You running away from school for good? Can I have your lunch pail?"

Colleen brushed past Brian and hurried down the path to meet Becky. "What's the matter, Becky?"

Becky held onto Colleen's arm as she tried to catch her breath. "I had to come up here fast to warn you."

"Warn me?" cried Colleen. "About what?" She stood on tiptoe and glanced over Becky's shoulder at the children playing outside the schoolhouse.

"Oh, no. Is Reverend going to give us a test?" asked Brian. "I'm not sure of my math sums and . . ."

"No. It's Laura McCoy," said Becky. "She's been busy all morning telling lies about you, Colleen. I tried to make her stop, but she just told me to shove an apple in my mouth."

Brian laughed as he walked past. "I wouldn't mind a candy apple. 'Sides, I already told Colleen Laura thinks she's dumb. Thinks she acts like a princess, too, but Ma says . . ."

"Hurry on to school, Brian," said Colleen. "I'll be right there."

The two girls stood silently until Brian was yards ahead.

"Brian told me at breakfast that Laura thinks I'm stuck up now that I'm living with Dr. Mike," Colleen said slowly. "I told him that it wasn't so." Colleen nudged her friend with her elbow. "You

8

don't think I've changed any since my ma died, do you, Becky? Tell me the truth."

" 'Course you haven't. And that's the truth all right." Becky smiled as she linked her arm through Colleen's and pulled her along the lane. "You were always nice to your ma and always smart in school. Since your ma died, you're nice to Dr. Mike and you're *still* the smartest girl in the whole class. Probably the best speller in the whole state."

Colleen grinned. "I don't know about that. Missy and Paul are very smart, and so are you, and . . ." Colleen stopped. "Dr. Mike thinks the reason Laura is acting so mean-spirited right now is because she's new to town." Colleen sighed. "I'm still not happy she's talking about me. But you have to admit Laura is very good with sums and figuring."

Becky gave a short laugh. "Laura is good with *figures* all right. She's figuring out a way to make the whole school turn against you."

Colleen started walking faster. "What did I ever do to her?"

Becky laughed as she hurried to catch up. "Hey, Laura is jealous, that's all."

Colleen smiled. "Come on. We'd better hurry before we're late. I don't want the Reverend to get upset with the class today."

"I'm so excited about the spelling bee. I studied my word list a zillion times last night."

"Me, too. Becky, as soon as Reverend rings the lunch bell, meet me by the swings. Laura will forget about me soon enough."

"Sure," agreed Becky. "By lunch Laura will be busy making someone else miserable."

Colleen grabbed onto Becky's hand and the two girls raced down the lane to the school. With so much to look forward to, Colleen didn't want a dull, heavy anchor like Laura McCoy to weigh down her morning.

3

Colleen could feel the tension in the air as soon as she and Becky entered the schoolhouse. Most of the little kids were in their seats, but the older kids were leaning against the chalkboard, arms crossed and wearing smug expressions. They looked as if they were waiting for some sort of show to begin.

"Look at Richard and Dillon," whispered Becky. "Richard looks like the cat who just swallowed a canary."

Laura was over by the potbellied stove, waving her hands in the air, talking to three other girls by the open window. As Colleen and Becky walked down the aisle, Laura turned, frowned, and then resumed talking a mile a minute to her captive audience.

"Hi, Becky," called Alice from the center of the crowd. "Hi, Colleen."

Colleen smiled broadly at Alice. "Hi, Alice. Are you ready for the spelling bee?"

Alice rolled her eyes and sighed. "No chance of me seeing Weisport. I tried to memorize the word list, but I just can't." Alice shook back her hair and smiled over at where the boys were standing. "Besides, Richard and Paul rode over last night to see our new kittens and I forgot all about the words."

Becky sighed next to Colleen. She had a huge crush on Richard and hated hearing about him flirting with every girl in the school. She slid into her seat and pulled Colleen down next to her. "Let's study our spelling words and just ignore the whole lot of them," whispered Becky.

Colleen nodded, busying herself with unstrapping her books. "All right. The spelling bee will be starting soon," Colleen said softly. "Once that gets going, everyone will start thinking about other things."

Reverend Johnson hurried into the schoolhouse and closed the door. "Good morning, class. Take your seats."

"When will we have the spelling bee, Reverend?" asked Laura. "Can we have it before lunch?"

"*May* we have it before lunch," Reverend corrected.

Laura raised one eyebrow and stuck her hand on her hip. "Oh, well, excuse me. I guess my mother is too busy sweeping out the *saloon* to teach me proper."

Reverend Johnson picked up a book and sat

down carefully on the edge of the desk. "You are being raised by a fine, churchgoing lady, Miss McCoy. There is nothing wrong with an honest day's work. As your teacher, it is my job to help you all with English grammar. Now, everyone please take your seats."

Colleen kept her eyes down on her desk as Laura walked past. She could hear Laura flop down in her seat, slamming books on her desktop.

"Settle down, class," called out Reverend in a stern voice. "Get out your math sums, children. While I work with the older children, I want Brian and Eric to put their first two problems on the board, please."

Colleen was reaching for her paper when Laura kicked her seat. Colleen turned around and found Laura glaring at her.

"Let's hurry with our sums, so Reverend will start talking about the spelling bee," said Becky. She reached into her desk and pulled out her tablet.

Colleen pulled out her tablet, then watched as a pale yellow scarf slid out of her desk and onto her lap. "Oh, my . . . look at this!"

"Wow, that's beautiful!" cried Becky. "Is it new?"

"It's not mine," stammered Colleen. She picked it up and handed it to Becky. "It was in my desk."

"Girls!" Reverend Johnson turned from the chalkboard to frown at Colleen and Becky.

Becky thrust the scarf back into Colleen's hands. "It's not mine."

"But it isn't mine either!" said Colleen. "I've never seen it before."

Reverend frowned again and set his chalk down. Every head turned to stare at Colleen.

"Is there a problem, girls?" asked Reverend. He walked down the aisle and picked up the scarf. "Should we put this in the cloakroom where it won't be so distracting?"

"It was in my desk," stammered Colleen, standing quickly. "I . . . I just . . . ."

"Hey!" Alice cried, scrambling out of her seat. "That's my scarf. I brought it today to show during history. It came straight from China!"

Reverend Johnson held the scarf toward Alice. As it dangled, the yellow scarf twirled, exposing a huge black ink stain.

Alice raced to Reverend Johnson and grabbed the scarf. "What happened? Colleen, you ruined it! What did you do?"

Colleen took a step back. "Nothing. I . . . I just found it in my desk."

"You hid it in your desk!" snapped Alice. She scratched at the spot. "This is ink. It will never come out!"

Reverend Johnson examined the scarf. "Maybe your mother could wash it, Alice."

"You can't wash silk!" exploded Alice. "It's fancy China silk." Alice wadded the scarf in her fist. "Oh, Colleen Cooper! Just wait til̄ mother about this!"

"But Colleen didn't do it," said Becky. "It j fell out of her desk."

"She hid it after she ruined it!" cried Alice, shaking the scarf up and down. "Are you telling me this scarf has legs and just walked over to Colleen's desk?"

"I just reached my hand in and there it was," explained Colleen. Colleen turned and nodded toward Laura. "You saw me find it just now, didn't you, Laura?"

Laura shrugged and shot Colleen a bored look. "I didn't see nothing."

"You didn't see *anything*," corrected the Reverend.

Laura sighed. As soon as Reverend looked away, she kicked Colleen's chair again.

"Maybe a robber put it in Colleen's desk," offered Brian.

Alice buried her face in the scarf, moaning more loudly.

"Ah, don't fret none, Alice," said Richard. "Once the trains start running, you'll have a sack full of silk scarves."

"I don't want a new scarf. This scarf was a present." Alice moaned again and her shoulders started to shake. Colleen felt terrible. The way Reverend was staring at her, he seemed to believe Alice.

15

"Go get the sheriff," suggested Richard. "Colleen is probably wanted in two or three towns for scarf staining."

"That will be enough," Reverend said shortly. "Alice, we are sorry about the scarf. Inquiries will be made at a later date. But, for right now, everyone be seated."

"Ain't Colleen going to get in trouble over this?" asked Laura.

"Be quiet, Miss McCoy." Reverend Johnson closed his eyes. He drew in several deep breaths before he turned and walked back toward the chalkboard.

"I'm sorry about your scarf, Alice," said Colleen.

"Take your seat, Colleen," said Reverend. "You two may discuss this after school."

Alice spun on her heel and walked back to her seat. Colleen sank into her own seat, her eyes glued to her desk top. She didn't want to look up. It seemed like the whole class must be staring at her.

After a few minutes, Colleen picked up her pencil, then set it back down again. Who ruined the beautiful scarf and then put it in her desk? Had Alice? Why would she do that?

"Don't think about it anymore," Becky said softly.

Colleen nodded, knowing she would be thinking about it for the rest of the day. How could she not think about it? She would talk to Alice about it after school. They were friends. Surely Alice would believe her when she got a chance to explain. But there was someone sitting in the school-room right now who disliked her so much they wanted her in trouble. Someone wanted to watch her twist and swing like a fly caught up in a mysterious web. Who could it be?

4

The rest of the morning crawled by. Colleen did her math sums, then listened halfheartedly as the younger children read their poems. Every once in a while Alice would turn around and frown at Colleen. Colleen never bothered to frown back. She felt terrible inside. She hated being judged, especially when she was so innocent.

Part of Colleen was just pure mad. Reverend Johnson had known her since she was a baby. She hadn't been a troublemaker. Besides, Reverend Johnson was the teacher and a sworn-in man of God. Colleen hadn't read through the whole Bible yet, but she knew God didn't want the Reverend to brand someone guilty without hearing both sides of the story.

Colleen refused to look at Alice, Laura, and smart-alecky Richard for the rest of the morning. Laura kicked the back of Colleen's chair three times during science, but Colleen just stared straight ahead.

"All right, class, put away your papers and pencils," Reverend said. "It is time to begin the spelling bee competition. I want you to count off starting with Jeremiah, and then all the odds stand by the right-hand windows, all the evens in front of the left windows."

Colleen and Becky exchanged disappointed glances. They sat right beside each other, so they would be on opposite teams.

As the students divided themselves in half, Colleen grew more and more anxious. Not only was Becky on the other team, but Colleen would be on the same side as Richard and Laura. It would be harder to concentrate on spelling when she was surrounded by people who disliked her.

Becky patted Colleen's shoulder. "We may still both end up in Weisport. Reverend Johnson said the last two students standing get to go."

At the beginning of the spelling bee, the Reverend took words from a red folder. The words were fairly easy. Colleen and Becky grinned and waved to each other from across the room. Only the Blakefield twins misspelled their words. As soon as they sat down, Reverend Johnson reached in his center desk drawer and pulled out a blue folder.

The words in the blue folder were *hard!*

With fewer than seven words, ten students were knocked out of the spelling bee. Colleen took her time and spelled *identity* correctly. Becky stammered and almost missed spelling *dubious*. As Becky tried to decide between an *I* and an *E*, Colleen closed her eyes tight and willed Becky to pick the *I*.

"D-U-B-I-U," Becky stopped and held up both hands. "Wait a minute, I mean, D-U-B-I, yes, definitely an I-O-U-S."

Reverend Johnson smiled. "Correct."

"Well, it took you long enough," complained Laura. "Reverend, I don't think the teachers in Weisport are going to let Becky take two hours to spell a word."

"Reverend wants us to take our time," said Becky.

Laura shrugged. "At the rate we're going now, the railroad's gonna run through this town before we get through with this spelling bee."

"That's enough!" Reverend Johnson tapped the yardstick on the front desk. "I will not allow this bickering to continue."

Brian waved his hand from his seat. "Reverend Johnson, since I already missed my word, do you mind if I just go home? Sully might take me fishin'."

Several children agreed that they should return home as well.

Reverend shook his head. "No. But since you seem to be restless, why don't you children at your seats copy down today's words from the chalkboard."

After ten more words, three students took their seats. Colleen looked around the room. Only five students were left. Becky, Richard, Paul, Colleen, and Laura McCoy.

"Maybe you should just send five of us to Weisport," suggested Becky.

Reverend Johnson smiled. "I wish I could. But we only have funds to send two students and one chaperone. Miss Dorothy has agreed to go, and then write a fine article for *The Gazette*."

Reverend Johnson put down the blue folder and got out a thin green folder. "These words have been sent to me from the judges in Weisport. I advise you all to take your time because these words are more difficult than those on our usual spelling list. So, once again, *take your time*."

Laura groaned. "But don't take *all day*, Becky."

Becky's cheeks flushed red, but she didn't look over at Laura.

Richard took his time, but went down on *synonym*. Paul misspelled *precision*.

"Well, well. It looks like Colorado Springs will be represented by the ladies," said Reverend Johnson.

Colleen and Becky each crossed their fingers and grinned at each other. It would be so much fun to take the stage to Weisport together!

"All right, ladies. Here we go. Becky, spell *presumptuousness*."

"What?" cried Becky. "I've never even heard of that word! Are you sure it is a word, Reverend?"

Reverend Johnson laughed. "Yes, I am *quite* sure. It means arrogant self-confidence."

"Sounds like Laura McCoy to me," called Richard from his seat.

"Be quiet, you poor loser!" snapped Laura.

"Children!" Reverend Johnson stood up and crossed his arms. "We are all on the same team in this school. Now I want this bickering to stop. If I hear one more word, I will start suspending students from this class. Do you understand?"

"Yes, sir," said Richard.

"Yes, sir," added Laura.

Becky bit her lip. "Could you please repeat my word, Reverend? Slowly?"

"Pre-sump-tu-ous-ness."

"P-R-E-S-U-M-P-" Becky stopped and licked her lips. "T-O-" Becky stopped again, saying the letters softly to herself.

Don't forget the U, Colleen wanted to shout. She kept her head down and chanted U-U-U over and over again in her head.

"P-R-E-S-U-M-P-T-U-I-O-U-S-N-E-S-S!"

22

Becky looked worried, then smiled at the Reverend. "Okay?"

"Not okay," said Laura.

"I'm sorry, Becky," Reverend said softly. "But you did an excellent job today."

Colleen clapped for Becky and was glad when the rest of the class joined in.

"Does that mean I win?" asked Laura.

"Not necessarily," pointed out Reverend Johnson. "If you and Colleen both spell your words correctly, you will both go to Weisport."

"Together?" asked Colleen.

"With Miss Dorothy," added Reverend. "But, if you misspell your word, then we will have Becky stand up again, and we will give each of you a new word."

Colleen clasped her hands and smiled at Becky. It would be wonderful if Laura missed her word!

"All right now. Let me find the next word for Miss McCoy." Reverend Johnson ran his finger down the list.

Find a hard one, Colleen prayed.

"Laura, spell *inconvenient*."

Colleen's heart sank. Laura's word didn't seem nearly as hard as Becky's had been.

Laura didn't even pause before answering. "I-N-C-O-N-V-E-N-I-E-N-T!"

Reverend smiled. "Correct." He glanced down at his list and then turned to Colleen. "Miss Cooper, please spell *retaliation*."

Dillon groaned. "What kind of word is that, Reverend?"

"It means to counterattack, to get even with someone for something they have done." Reverend turned back to Colleen. "If someone does you a wrong, you try to get revenge, to retaliate." The Reverend cleared his throat. "Of course, God does not want us to retaliate. All right now, Colleen, please spell *retaliation*."

Colleen swallowed. "Retaliation. R-E-T-A-L-I-A-T-I-O-N!"

Reverend Johnson stood up and clapped. "Correct. Looks like we have our finalists for the spelling bee in Weisport."

"Congratulations!" Becky called out from her seat.

Colleen caught Becky's smile. Then Colleen locked eyes with Laura McCoy. Laura smiled, too. But hers wasn't a warm, friendly smile like Becky's. Laura's smile was pure mean.

5

On Friday morning, Sully got the buggy ready, and Brian and Dr. Mike drove Colleen into town to catch the stage to Weisport.

"Bye, Sully!" cried Colleen as they started off. "See you Sunday night."

"Are you sure you packed everything?" asked Dr. Mike. "Did you pin your money sock to your petticoat?"

"Yes, Ma. I have three dresses, an extra pair of shoes, nightgown, toothbrush, and lots of warm stockings." Colleen lifted a corner of her skirt. "And my ticket and money are safe."

Brian tried to pick up Colleen's suitcase. "This weighs a ton, Colleen. How long are you going to be gone?"

"I'll be home in three days, Brian," laughed Colleen. "Do you want me to bring you anything?"

"Yeah, bring me some gold dust. Petey says that his dad is real rich somewhere. Every time he sticks his pan in the stream, he pulls up another gold nugget." Brian pulled on Colleen's sleeve. "Ask Laura what kind of pan her dad has and then get me one of those, okay?"

"I didn't even know Laura and Petey had a dad," said Colleen. "But, I'll ask, Brian. If I can't find a pan, I'll bring you back some candy."

Dr. Mike smiled. "Did you ever hear the story about the man who got rich from selling pans?"

Colleen shook her head. "Mr. Bray sells his cake pans for twenty cents. You'd have to sell an awful lot to get rich."

"Well, I heard that when gold was discovered in the American River in California, a man named Brennan heard about it before news got out. So Mr. Brennan bought all the tin pans he could find. Hundreds of them. Then he raced through the streets with a bottle of gold dust, crying, 'Gold discovered down by Sutter's Mill!' The next thing you knew, people were crowding his store to buy the pans that he sold for sixteen dollars apiece!"

Brian and Colleen laughed. Dr. Mike always had the best stories.

"That's terrible," cried Colleen.

"That's smart!" laughed Brian. "Ma, you should sell your medicine for a hundred dollars a spoonful. Then we'd be the richest people in town."

Dr. Mike turned and tugged Brian's hat down over his eyes. "I'm supposed to *help* people, Brian. The people in town are part of our family."

Colleen glanced over at Dr. Mike. "I don't think

Laura McCoy thinks of me as family, Dr. Mike. In fact, if Miss Dorothy telegraphs you that I am missing, be sure and have the sheriff arrest Laura."

"Richard said Laura put that scarf in your desk. He said he saw her trying it on before school," reported Brian.

"Well, whatever happened at school, Colleen, I want you to relax and concentrate on having a wonderful time in Weisport," said Dr. Mike.

"I will." Colleen picked up her bonnet. Dr. Mike had lent it to her for the trip. It had been Dr. Mike's favorite since Sully had picked it out for her in Boston. Colleen felt the satin ties against her fingertips. She was lucky to be living with Dr. Mike and Sully. Since her mother's death, Colleen and her brothers had been to Boston and Washington to meet President Grant. No one else in Colorado Springs had ever traveled so far.

Dr. Mike pulled the buggy up in front of Bray's General Store. Brian hopped out and grabbed the reins.

"I'll tie up for you, Ma. When I'm finished, can I go inside and get a piece of candy?" asked Brian.

"Just one, Brian. And could you ask Miss Dorothy if she needs any help with her suitcase?"

Colleen put on her bonnet and smiled while Dr. Mike tied it for her. She was starting to get excited about the trip. Maybe traveling with Laura wouldn't be so bad after all. Dr. Mike had packed a huge basket of fruit and sandwiches. And early this morning, Matthew's fiancée, Ingrid, had dropped off a dozen apple cookies.

"You look wonderful, Colleen." Dr. Mike reached over and hugged Colleen tightly. "Promise me you will send a telegram the moment you reach Weisport."

"I promise," said Colleen as she hugged Dr. Mike back.

As Colleen climbed out of the buggy, she heard footsteps behind her. She turned and watched as Laura McCoy and Petey came racing down the street. Laura was wearing the blue dress she usually wore to church on Sunday, but Colleen had never seen the small straw hat with the brightly painted flowers around the rim. Petey was carrying a small, worn-looking carpetbag.

"Morning, Laura. What a perfectly beautiful hat," exclaimed Dr. Mike. "Where did you get it?"

Laura barely glanced at Dr. Mike before answering. "From my closet."

Colleen cringed, but Dr. Mike did not react with anything but a laugh. "Hello, Petey. How nice of you to help your sister." Dr. Mike looked down the street. "Is your mother coming down to see you off? I wanted to talk to her."

The smile left Laura's face. "About what?"

Colleen and Dr. Mike glanced at each other. Colleen held her suitcase more tightly. Maybe now Dr. Mike would understand how horrible Laura McCoy could be.

Dr. Mike took the basket out of the back of the buggy. "I just wanted to let her know that as soon as Colleen telegraphs me, I'll let her know. To make sure of your safe arrival."

Laura shrugged. "Don't bother with none of that. If the sheriff doesn't come to call, then there's no trouble. No news is good news as far as we're concerned."

Petey nodded. "What's in the basket, Dr. Mike?"

"Cookies, fruit." Dr. Mike lifted back the checkered napkin. "Cheese sandwiches. I packed enough for everyone, Laura. Plenty for you, Miss Dorothy and . . ."

"I've got my own food. I won't be needing yours," Laura said. She took her bag from Petey. "Bye, Petey. Tell Ma I'll see her in a few days."

Petey glanced over at the basket. "You ain't got no food, Laura, 'ceptin' that butter bread Ma . . ."

"Git on with you," Laura said quickly. "Too much food on a trip can make you sick. Everyone knows that."

Petey stood quiet for a second, then hugged Laura around the waist. "I'll miss you."

Laura bent down and kissed the top of Petey's head. "Miss you, too. Now go help Ma."

"I'd better see what's keeping Miss Dorothy,"

Dr. Mike said cheerfully. "The stage should be here any minute."

"Ma!"

Brian rushed out of Bray's front door. "Ma! Come quick."

"What's wrong, Brian?" asked Colleen.

Brian raced over and grabbed Dr. Mike's hand. "Ma! It's Miss Dorothy. She tripped coming off the stool. Mr. Bray said she hurt her leg real bad!"

Dr. Mike reached into the back of the buggy, grabbed her medical bag, and hurried after Brian.

"Girls, I'll be back. Hold the stagecoach!" called Dr. Mike.

As Dr. Mike disappeared into the general store, the stagecoach pulled around the corner by the post office.

Laura squinted up at the sun. "Right on time."

"Yeah. I hope Miss Dorothy is okay. What if she can't make the trip after all?"

Laura gave Colleen a crooked grin. "Well, I guess you'll have to get on the stage with your fancy basket and adorable bonnet and ride without any adult to hold your hand."

Colleen blushed, suddenly feeling very over-dressed in Dr. Mike's bonnet. "I just meant that we need a chaperone, and . . ."

Laura dusted off her faded bag. "Correction, Colleen. *You* need a chaperone. I don't need anyone but myself. So I guess I'll be just fine."

"Colleen, Ma needs you!" called Brian from the

30

second floor above the general store. "Go to the icehouse and bring back some ice for Miss Dorothy's leg."

Colleen dropped her suitcase. "Tell her I'll get some."

"Colleen, Ma needs you!" mimicked Laura. "What a joke. Dr. Mike isn't your *real* ma, Colleen. Who are you trying to kid?"

Laura's words pounded against Colleen, leaving her face bright red. "I'm not trying to *kid* anyone, Laura. You're right, Dr. Mike isn't my mother. But Brian likes to call her that, okay?"

Laura held up both hands. "Of course it's okay, Colleen. I guess whatever you all want to do in this crummy town is okay from now on — now that you have the wonderful Dr. Mike as your new ma."

Colleen dropped her bag and spun around. She glanced up at the window and lowered her voice. "Are you trying to make me feel guilty about something, Laura? It's not *my* fault my mother died. Do you think I'm glad she died, just so I could live with Dr. Mike and Sully?" Colleen started to say more, but just shook her head. Why bother? She walked towards the icehouse, too mad to try and talk to Laura anymore. Laura McCoy had to be the meanest girl in the entire West. Maybe in the world!

6

Miss Dorothy had sprained her leg so badly, she could not go to Weisport to chaperone the girls. Reverend Johnson hurried over from the school, but insisted he couldn't travel because he had to finish teaching school on Friday and preach the sermon on Sunday.

"We'll be fine," insisted Laura. She kicked the end of her bag and sighed. "We should be halfway there by now."

Colleen gripped her own basket, wondering if she wouldn't have more fun staying home and doing chores than traveling in a stage alone with Laura McCoy.

"You girls are far too young to travel without a chaperone," said Dr. Mike. "Isn't there anyone free to travel to the spelling bee in Weisport?"

"They'll be fine, Dr. Mike," the Reverend assured her. "It's less than a day by stage. And besides, Lucille Potts will be on the stage, too."

"I'm going," declared Laura flatly. She opened the door and got inside. "I won the spelling bee and I'm going."

Dr. Mike looked concerned. She glanced toward the saloon. "Laura, maybe we should alert your mother to the change in plans."

Laura leaned back in her seat and shook her head. "She won't care. Let's get going."

"Colleen will be okay, Ma," added Brian.

"My daughter will be thinkin' the Indians got me," complained Mrs. Potts, walking toward the group. "Is this stage leaving today or not?"

Colleen reached up and hugged Dr. Mike. "I'll be fine, Dr. Mike. I'll telegraph you as soon as I get there. It's not nearly as far as Denver, and like Reverend said, Mrs. Potts will be on the stage, too."

Mrs. Potts looked alarmed. "I'm not going to be in charge of anybody but myself."

The stage master laughed. "We'll be there before dark. Now come on, ladies. We're late enough."

Colleen quickly kissed Dr. Mike and Brian and got aboard before Dr. Mike could change her mind. The last thing she wanted right now was to have the trip canceled. Laura would beat the Reverend back to school to let everyone know that Colleen Cooper couldn't travel alone.

"Have fun. Be careful!" Dr. Mike called as the stage pulled away.

Colleen stared out the window, watching Colorado Springs get smaller and smaller. When it was no more than a dark smudge, she opened her basket and got out her diary.

Dear Diary,

Well, at last the journey to Weisport has begun. I am very sorry that Miss Dorothy hurt her leg. Not only is she an interesting lady, but I was counting on her to sit between Laura and me on the stage. Actually, I don't have to worry about that since Laura is sitting next to Mrs. Potts. Nobody is talking to one another. Laura is reading a book and Mrs. Potts fell asleep as soon as we left town. Oh, well, quiet is better than a noisy argument. I hope the peace lasts till we return. The only thing I know about Weisport is that there is a lot of talk about the new railroad station that will be built. It is going to be so fancy. Once, while Ma was still alive, Matthew and I drew our favorite sketches of what a really fancy train station might look like. Ma would be proud that I'm traveling alone. She always said that I had a good head on my shoulders. I guess between Ma and Dr. Mike, I know that a woman can take care of herself just fine.

"Are you writing your word list?" asked Laura.

"What?" Colleen's head jerked up and she pressed her diary close to her chest.

"Are you writing your words for the spelling bee?" asked Laura.

Colleen shook her head. "Just writing in my diary. I thought I'd like a reminder of the trip."

Laura raised an eyebrow. "What is there to tell? So far it's been as dull as dishwater. Unless maybe I missed something exciting?"

"No," Colleen closed her book, beginning to feel a little foolish. "I just like to write."

Laura picked up her book. "I like to read."

Colleen shoved the diary into the side of her basket. "Oh, I do, too. I can hardly wait till we get more books for the library in town. I think I've read most all of them."

"Me, too," said Laura. "I'm almost finished with this."

Colleen smiled. "Mark Twain. You have a copy of *The Celebrated Jumping Frog*. Did you know Mark Twain has three daughters and they put on plays each Saturday? They write some of the plays themselves and, of course, their father . . ."

Laura lowered her book. "How do you know all that?"

"Dr. Mike told me. Her mother read a great article about Twain in Boston and sent the clipping to us. Did you know that sometimes Mr. Twain stops writing a story for a year or two and never goes back to it till the story is ready to tell itself?"

"Yes, I know that," Laura said. "Did you know Mark Twain spent a night in jail with killers and thieves?"

"He did not!" cried Colleen. Surely Dr. Mike would have told her about that.

"Did you know how his brother Henry was killed about ten years ago? It was a horrible, violent death."

"You're making all of this up, Laura. I should have never mentioned that I liked Mark Twain, and then you would have let the poor man alone."

Laura leaned back in her seat and turned a page. "What I am saying is the truth, Colleen. It isn't my fault that you have to wait for all of your news to come from Boston."

"I don't," snapped Colleen. "Last year Reverend read us a little from Mark Twain's newest book, *The Innocents Abroad*, and he didn't mention a single word about the author being in jail. Back East, people are paying him a hundred dollars a night just to give a speech. So don't think you know everything, 'cause you don't."

Laura glanced over at Mrs. Potts before leaning forward to hiss, "The school I went to before this dumb school was *in* the East, so I guess I know ten times more than you'll know any day of the week." Laura flopped back in her seat, picking up her book and holding it an inch from her nose.

Colleen sat back as well, grabbing her diary and writing as fast as she could. She had nothing to say, but she didn't want Laura to know that. The faster she scribbled, the more she thought about Mark Twain. She loved his books. There was no way he ever spent time in jail, either. Laura had to tack on some pure mean thing to say about everyone who seemed to be the least bit happy. Colleen wrote another page of scribble and then smiled, hoping Laura would think she was having a perfectly wonderful time on her trip. Colleen smiled so hard her back teeth were beginning to ache. Oh, that Laura McCoy! Thanks to her, Colleen was going to have to drive herself crazy with wondering what ever happened to Mark Twain's poor brother, Henry.

7

By the time the stage stopped to water the horses and allow the passengers to freshen up, Colleen and Laura were not speaking to each other.

"Twenty-minute rest stop," called out the driver. "Freshen up and grab some grub. Come on, ladies. Time to stretch your legs."

Colleen was helped off the stage after Mrs. Lucille Potts. Laura refused the offered hand of the stage master and hopped off herself.

"Mercy, I am far too old to be traveling all day," declared Mrs. Potts, dusting herself off as she rearranged her skirts. "If my youngest girl hadn't had those twins, I would be sitting on my front porch right now."

"How long has your daughter lived in Weisport?" asked Colleen.

Mrs. Potts retied her bonnet before answering. "She married a second cousin of Mr. Bray's and left a year ago spring. Now she has two little babies. I promised her I would stay a week, but no more. I am too old for babies." Mrs. Potts stepped up onto the porch of the inn. "I am also too old to listen to young girls squabble over Mark Twain."

"Sorry to have disturbed you," mumbled Colleen.

Laura picked up a stone and sent it skittering across the dirt yard. "It's a free country. I paid for my ticket. Same as you."

"Seems to me Reverend Johnson could have found two girls who could both *spell* and *behave* to send to Weisport," declared Mrs. Potts, fanning herself with her hanky. She ambled up to the inn door and let the door close on Colleen and Laura. Both girls glanced at each other.

"I thought she was asleep," Colleen said softly.

"Maybe we can bribe the driver to leave now," whispered Laura. She slid onto a bench and lifted her face to the sun. "Feels good to be out of that stage. My backside is sore."

"Mine, too." Colleen stretched. "Not too much longer. I hope our rooms are nice."

"Our *room*, you mean," corrected Laura. "Reverend told Ma that we may be three or four to a room."

Colleen sank down onto the bench beside Laura. "You're kidding. We'd have more room if we just slept in the stage."

Laura raised one eyebrow. "I think we've spent

enough time together in the stage, Princess. Besides, sharing a room for two nights will not kill you."

Colleen frowned at Laura. "My name is not Princess. And actually, Laura, I *did* share a room with Brian. Sometimes, my older brother was crowded in there with us, too."

Laura laughed. "Gosh, did your temper come with that bonnet?"

Colleen opened the inn door and walked inside. She was surprised when Laura stood up and followed her. After freshening up, both girls waited outside in the shade for the stage driver.

Colleen got her basket from the stage. She was so hungry all of a sudden! She carefully placed her diary on the bottom and got an apple. She thought about offering something to Laura, but she was getting tired of Laura's making fun of her about everything. Out of the corner of her eye, Colleen watched Laura unwrap a thick slice of bread from a checkered napkin. She spread the thick square of butter with her little finger, and bit into it.

Colleen finished her apple and took out a cheese sandwich. Dr. Mike had tied the sandwich with a bright scrap of red ribbon. By the second bite, Colleen softened. Dr. Mike wouldn't want her to be so selfish, even if Laura did deserve a taste of her own medicine.

"Laura, are you hungry?" asked Colleen. "Dr.

Mike packed enough for an army. Here, try an orange. Dr. Mike's mother shipped them all the way from Boston."

Laura shook her head. "Ma packed me some bread, shipped all the way from the saloon kitchen."

Colleen kicked the tiny pebbles by her feet. "Let me know if I ever say anything that *doesn't* offend you."

"I'll do that." Laura crossed her arms, leaning against the tree and watching the clouds. "Was your ma the first person you knew who died?"

Colleen's head jerked up. For one brief second she felt exposed, as if Laura had been reading her diary.

Laura didn't wait for an answer. "My older sister died about six years ago. Then my ma."

"Your ma?" Colleen stood up so fast her sandwich and apple core fell into the dust. No wonder Mrs. McCoy didn't walk Laura to the stagecoach. "Why didn't you tell us? I feel so terrible, and . . ."

Laura took another bite of her bread. "Not Ma. She's my grandmother. Once my real ma took sick, Papa wired my grandmother to come east to take care of us."

"Boston?"

Laura shook her head. "Pittsburgh. Then my ma died, and Papa took off for the gold rush. He said he'd send for us, but he never did. After six months, Ma packed us up to come back here. She loves the West. Says everyone has a chance to start over here."

"Dr. Mike feels the same way," said Colleen. She took a step closer and put her hand on Laura's shoulder. "I'm real sorry about your ma, Laura."

Laura shrugged, standing up so fast Colleen's hand flew off. "Don't. People die. Some of us get the fairy-tale ending, like you. Your ma dies, you end up in a nice house with someone smart and respectable like Dr. Mike. And now you even got a dad."

"I'm sorry, Laura." Colleen was going to tell Laura that her pa had left too, but she didn't want to jump in on her story. Colleen knew Laura would just remind her that she ended up with Dr. Mike and Laura ended up living above a saloon.

"All aboard!" called the stage master.

Using her foot, Laura pushed herself from the tree.

"Now don't go dopey on me and think I told you all this so you would feel sorry for me."

Colleen hurried to catch up. "Why did you tell me?"

Laura shrugged. "Mrs. Potts, I guess."

"Mrs. Potts? Our traveling companion?"

"Yeah, she smells like vinegar and garlic. Maybe she has an herb bag tied around her neck or something. But she smells. I can't sit next to her anymore. It's like sitting next to a very large salad!"

Colleen picked up her basket. "Want to sit next to me?"

"Okay. Anything is better than Mrs. Potts."

"Hurry up, girls," called the stage master. "Mrs. Potts, we're ready to start."

"Wait for me!" cried Mrs. Potts from the front porch. "These are old legs I'm standing on."

The stage master opened the door and Laura climbed in first. She moved Colleen's basket and books to the right and sat down in Colleen's seat by the window. Colleen got in and sat beside Laura, making sure her skirt did not take up too much room. Finally Mrs. Potts got in and heaved herself down into the center of the opposite seat.

"Well, now," said Mrs. Potts, folding her hands atop her large middle and smiling at both girls. "This is more like it. Now that you girls are wearing your best manners, the trip shall finally begin."

The stage master latched the door, and within seconds they were off. Colleen glanced over at her basket, wondering if she would be able to write any more in her diary with Laura sitting so close by. Laura slumped lower in her seat and closed her eyes as Mrs. Potts started to unwrap what smelled like a large onion sandwich.

Colleen stared out the window, feeling a million

new thoughts rush round her head. Laura had not had an easy life. But neither had Colleen. Her father had deserted her, too. Her mother had died. Awful, sad things happen in life sometimes. It doesn't mean that you have to turn into a nasty, rude person. Colleen leaned back in her seat. Both she and Laura had lost a mother to death and a father to the gold rush, but Colleen had been given to Dr. Mike and her world of medicine and warmth. Laura had been left in the care of a grandmother too busy sweeping and cooking in the saloon to pay attention to Petey and Laura.

As the stage picked up speed, it rocked Colleen back and forth. Colleen closed her eyes, but couldn't sleep. Laura was right. Colleen had gotten the fairy-tale ending. Why couldn't there be another happy ending for Laura?

8

"Looks like we'll be there in time for supper," said Colleen cheerfully. She leaned forward and stretched. "I think my back is ready for the trip to be over."

Mrs. Potts rubbed an apple up and down her sleeve. "Well, I've a bit more padding, but this is my last apple."

"You can always chew your garlic necklace," Laura said.

Colleen cringed, but Mrs. Potts just laughed. "Oh, you noticed my necklace, did you? Yes, I always travel with garlic. It keeps me healthy."

Laura nodded. "Well, my mother might disagree with you, Mrs. Potts."

"Oh, is that so?"

"Yes," said Laura. "She's a doctor. A very *good* doctor. My mother graduated from the Women's Medical College of Pennsylvania. I don't believe they offer a course in garlic."

"Maybe they should." Mrs. Potts' eyes darted from Colleen to Laura, then down at her feet, looking confused. "Your mothers are both medical doctors?"

Colleen looked at Laura, wondering what in the world she was up to now.

Laura laughed. "Yes. My mother is in New York now. Finding a cure for . . . for fleabites."

Mrs. Potts smiled. "Well, wait till I tell my daughter that I had such highfalutin traveling companions."

"That's probably why we fought a little," said Laura, smiling warmly now. "Sometimes we disagree over various medical procedures. Right, Colleen?"

"What?" Colleen had been so engrossed in the drama, she barely had time to recover. "I mean, yes."

"For instance," Laura went on, "when Miss Dorothy fell and hurt her leg, my mother would have wanted heat applied, while Dr. Quinn suggested ice."

Mrs. Potts' eyebrows rose up into her bonnet. "I use heat myself sometimes."

"The Indians heat rocks and they work well enough," said Laura.

Colleen stared out the window, not quite sure if she should keep her mouth shut or not.

"Well, this has turned out to be a nice trip after all," announced Mrs. Potts as the stage came to a stop. "I shall certainly tell my daughter that I was surrounded by knowledgeable girls."

Laura waited until Mrs. Potts had been helped off the stage. Then she leaned forward and smiled at Colleen. "See how much nicer she was the moment she found out I was the daughter of a *doctor*?"

Colleen shrugged. "She was nicer because you finally started to *talk* to her. That's all."

Laura grabbed up her carpetbag and smiled again. "So, you don't think people treat you nicer just because you are the daughter of Dr. Quinn?"

"Of course not." Colleen tried to keep her voice calm, but she felt annoyed.

"And you know people in Weisport will be extra nice to you once they find out that the marvelous Dr. Quinn is your new ma!"

Colleen grabbed her basket and tried to get out the door. "If I'm nice, people will be nice back. Believe me, Laura. It's that simple."

Colleen hurried away from the stage looking for the telegraph office.

Laura caught up to her and tapped Colleen's bonnet.

"What is it now, Laura?" Maybe she wanted to apologize.

"Want to try a little experiment? You should like it. Mark Twain would have *loved* it."

Colleen nodded. "Okay, what?"

"Let's trade places while we're in Weisport.

47

You be me, and I'll wear your bonnet and get to be you."

Colleen frowned. "That's silly. Besides, we're entering a contest."

"So what? They are expecting two students from Colorado Springs. We don't know anyone here."

"But why would we pretend to be each other?" Colleen's heart was beginning to pound so fast, she was afraid Laura would notice any minute.

Laura smiled, her eyes on the beautiful silk and lace bonnet. "Because I want to see what it feels like to have people like me right off the bat."

The frankness of Laura's words startled Colleen. She would have been able to dismiss Laura's normal lies, but the truth made Colleen reconsider. Had people been treating Colleen in a different way since she left the boardinghouse and moved into Dr. Mike's life?

"Maybe the thought of being Laura McCoy isn't good enough for you," Laura said. She swung her carpetbag to the other hand and started walking toward the hotel. "Forget it."

As Colleen watched her walk away, her heartbeat slowed. Was there any truth to what Laura said? Would people like her right away if they knew her mother scrubbed kitchen pots in a saloon instead of saving lives in a clinic?

"I'm the same person now as I was when I helped my mother in the rooming house," Colleen assured herself. "I haven't changed a bit. People like me for being me."

A sudden gust of dry wind swept across the street, rolling tumbleweed and robbing Laura, Colleen, and Mrs. Potts of their hats. They blew in wild circles into the street, tumbling along the edge of the walk.

As Colleen dropped her bag and hurried after her hat, she caught Laura's eye. There was no coldness now, only a weary, defeated look. Colleen decided then, in that brief moment, to bend down and pick up Laura's dusty straw hat.

9

Horace Bing raced out of the telegraph office and caught up with Dr. Mike as she headed into the general store.

"Safe and sound," Horace called out, waving the telegram. "No need to worry about Colleen, Dr. Mike."

Mr. Bray set his broom down and scowled at Horace. "Is there any such thing as privacy anymore, Horace?"

Dr. Mike laughed as she read the telegram. "Trip was fine. Colleen will see us Sunday."

"Bringing home the spelling bee trophy to boot," laughed Horace. "Reverend said Laura and Colleen can outspell anyone in Colorado."

"I hope so," said Dr. Mike. "I think I'll go tell Mrs. McCoy the girls are fine. It will give me a chance to introduce myself."

Mr. Bray picked up his broom and started to sweep again. "You'll have a hard time talking to *that* one. She comes in here once a month and buys flour and lard. That's about it."

Dr. Mike was surprised. "That's hardly enough to feed two growing children."

Horace shrugged, then scratched his head. "Myra met Mrs. McCoy when she first hit town. Said she's nice enough. Kind of young to be saddled with two grandkids."

"She isn't their mother?"

"I didn't know that," added Loren Bray. " 'Course nobody ever tells me anything. Seems if I didn't come outside to sweep the walk, I wouldn't know a darn thing that went on in this town."

"Thanks for the telegram, Horace." Dr. Mike handed Loren a list. "I'll be back for my supplies soon. Are the seed packets in yet?"

"Yes. Plenty to choose from."

"I'll send Myra and the baby down to get some, too," said Horace as he started to leave. "Maybe you can hold the baby while Myra takes a minute to plant those seeds, Loren."

Dr. Mike and Horace laughed as Mr. Bray scowled and went back inside.

Dr. Mike smoothed back her hair and brushed off her vest. She had been meaning to introduce herself to Mrs. McCoy for weeks. But every time she started to walk across the yard after church, the McCoys seemed to disappear.

Dr. Mike walked past the saloon's wooden-slatted doors and into the side alley. There were four barrels containing empty whiskey and ale bottles, but the stone walkway was swept clean and a washtub filled with geraniums sat by the stairs leading up to the rooms above the saloon. Dr. Mike wasn't sure if she should try the living quarters upstairs or use the back door and go into the kitchen where Mrs. McCoy worked as a cook. Since it was almost suppertime, she decided to try the kitchen.

"Hello!" Dr. Mike opened the back door and stuck her head inside. The large room was filled with steam and the faint odor of onions. Hank Claggerty, the saloon owner, liked his chili hot and packed with onions.

"Come on in," called a voice from the stove. "I'm stirring and not likely to stop."

Dr. Mike walked into the dimly lit kitchen, trying not to cough from the steam and heat. It had to be twenty degrees hotter inside than out on the street.

"Mrs. McCoy?" Dr. Mike set her medical bag down on the butcher-block stand and smiled.

Mrs. McCoy turned, squinting through the steam before she smiled. Then she dropped her spoon into the bubbling pot and grabbed her apron. "Oh, no. You're the doctor lady. It's not Petey, is it?"

Dr. Mike reached out and took her hand. "No,

no, Petey's fine. Probably out playing with my Brian. I just came by to tell you that Laura and Colleen have reached Weisport."

Mrs. McCoy breathed in a huge sigh of relief, her shoulders slumped. "Oh, thank the Lord. I told Laura that I thought a stagecoach trip was too much, her being only thirteen and all, but that girl has a steel will."

Dr. Mike pushed up her sleeves and smiled back. She glanced at the partially opened window. A trickle of sweat zigzagged down her spine. Mrs. McCoy brushed back her hair and hurried over to the window. She took a board and jammed it under the windowpane, lifting it another three inches.

"Can never get enough air in here when I'm making Hank's chili." She turned and pointed to a chair. "Please, Ma'am, sit down. Can I offer you some water?"

Dr. Quinn shook her head, then sank into the chair and nodded. "Yes, thank you. And please, call me Dr. Mike."

"Thank you. I heard the ladies at church calling you Dr. Mike. I told Petey and Laura that you sure are too pretty to have such a manly name." Mrs. McCoy smiled, and in the filtered sunlight, Dr. Mike could see the startling resemblance to her granddaughter, Laura. "You can call me Maudie."

"Nice to finally meet you, Maudie."

"Likewise, Dr. Mike. Now, let me get you

something cool before you need a doctor yourself. Those girls are going to have a fine time, don't you think?" Mrs. McCoy asked. She went to the sideboard and filled a glass to the top with water. "Here you go."

When Dr. Mike reached for the glass, she took hold of Mrs. McCoy's left hand. "You cut yourself."

Instantly, Maudie withdrew both hands as if scalded.

"Let me see. You're bleeding under your nails."

Maudie bit her lip, then hid her hands under her apron. "It's nothing, Dr. Mike. Please, don't mention none of this to Hank. He runs a clean kitchen in here, and I like the extra money I make cookin'."

Dr. Mike stood up and tried to take Maudie's hands. "I just want to see. Did you cut yourself, or are you chapped?"

Maudie shook her head, sending two huge tears down her cheeks. She held out both hands, then turned her face away. "I don't know what's wrong. I'm a clean woman, Dr. Mike. Sure, I live upstairs with the kids, and a saloon isn't a palace, but you can go up there and see how clean a place I keep. My grandkids wear clean clothes . . ."

Dr. Mike reached up and held Maudie's shoulder. "You are a very clean person, I'm sure, Maudie. Why, your Petey and Laura are lovely children. I just want to examine your hands. How

54

long have you been finding blood under your fingernails?"

Maudie shrugged. "Oh, a few weeks. First, I had a bruise on my arm. Thought I hit myself with a kettle once when I got in a hurry."

"May I see?"

Dr. Mike pushed up the cotton sleeve and studied the large purple mark on the inside of Maudie's arm.

"It don't hurt much," said Maudie. "I don't feel sick. Maybe a little tired, but with my work, I guess that's a likely feeling."

"Of course," said Dr. Mike. She looked around the kitchen. "Do you and the children eat all your meals here?"

Maudie nodded. "Here or upstairs. I don't like the kids sitting here if the saloon is filled up with a bad lot. If things get too noisy, I take them back upstairs. I read them the Bible while they eat. Saturdays I read that funny fella, Mark Twain."

"Nice idea." Dr. Mike glanced at her black medical bag. "And when do *you* eat?"

Maudie grinned. "Oh, I eat here and there." She glanced back over her shoulder. "Tasting these pots keeps me pretty full." A stricken look crossed her face. " 'Course, I never redip my spoon, Dr. Mike. Like I said, I'm a clean woman."

Dr. Mike laughed. "I only wish *I* knew how to cook."

Maudie bit her lip, glancing at the stove. "I

better get back to work. Hank will be in here any minute asking if the biscuits have been cut."

"Do you serve the children fruit or vegetables?" asked Dr. Mike.

Maudie nodded. "When I can get them, my kids get them."

"I know how infrequently Mr. Bray gets them in the store, and . . ."

"My kids eat good," said Maudie. She walked over and picked up a new spoon. "I take good care of my girl's kids. Just like I promised."

"I'm sure you do," Dr. Mike assured her. "I'm just worried about the fruits, because . . ."

Maudie turned around, swatting the steam with her spoon. "Because why, Dr. Mike? You thinking I can't take proper care of my grandkids?"

"I was more worried about you."

Maudie waved her spoon in dismissal. "Don't worry about me. I'm past worrying about."

Dr. Mike shook her head. "No. No, you're not, Maudie. I'm worried about your bleeding and the bruises."

"I'll heal." Maudie banged down the lid to the pot.

"You will if you start taking better care of yourself," explained Dr. Mike. She was trying to be gentle, but she could tell by the way Maudie's spine was beginning to stiffen that she had worn out her welcome.

Maudie turned slowly from the stove. She

wasn't smiling now. "I've done real good all by myself for a long, long time, Dr. Mike."

Dr. Mike picked up her bag, but remained standing in the center of the hot, steamy kitchen. "I'd like to examine you in the clinic, Maudie. We need to talk."

Maudie turned back around and gave a short, hard laugh. "I'm too busy working to talk anymore. You'll have to excuse me now."

"We have to talk, Maudie. I don't want to alarm you, but it's important."

Maudie sighed and set the spoon down with a thunk. "Talk now, Dr. Mike. The supper crowd is waitin' on their biscuits."

Dr. Mike walked to the stove and put her hand on Maudie's arm. "You're bleeding under your nails because you are lacking in some very important nutrients, Maudie. It's serious."

Maudie laughed. "Hey, I'm lacking in a fancy ranch and a horse and buggy, too. So what else is new? I'll eat a bowl of this chili and get all the nutrients I need."

"You have scurvy, Maudie."

Maudie looked alarmed. "Scurvy?"

"Yes, and unless it's treated, you will get progressively worse, and . . ."

Maudie put her hands on her hips. "You saying I have some sort of *disease*? All that's wrong is my hands are chapped from me working from dawn till dusk."

57

"It's nothing to be ashamed of, Maudie. Our brave soldiers often got scurvy and people on long ship voyages as well . . ."

Maudie gave a hard laugh. "Yeah, that's how I must have gotten it. On one of my long, sun-filled voyages around the world. Now you just turn around with your black bag full of bad news and get out of here right now. And if you tell Hank or one other soul about this, I will come after you, you hear me?" Maudie picked up the rolling pin and slammed it down on the floured board. "Get out of here with your telegrams and evil messages! I feel fine. I feel just fine!"

Dr. Mike bumped against the chairs as she headed for the door. "Scurvy is treatable. You need fruit and tomatoes!"

"Get out!" shouted Maudie.

Dr. Mike slid out the door and into the alley as Hank rushed into the kitchen.

"What in tarnation is going on in here?" he bellowed.

Dr. Mike leaned her head against the side of the wall and tried to catch her breath. If Maudie already had advanced scurvy, how safe were Laura and Petey in her care?

58

10

The large-boned man with curly red hair set the suitcases inside the hotel room and held out the key. "Here you go, ladies."

"Thank you." Laura stepped in front of Colleen, taking the key. "I appreciate your kindness."

The man grinned and nodded. "Good luck in the spelling bee, ladies. I have my own kid studying hard right now."

"Studying, now?" asked Colleen. She glanced at her basket. She hadn't looked at her words since she left Colorado Springs.

"He's a worker, that one," replied the man. "When I was his age I was too busy chasing the wild horses to worry much about schoolin'." He nodded again and left.

As soon as the door was closed, Colleen rummaged through her basket and brought out the word list. "We better get started, Laura. Maybe all of the contestants are studying hard this very minute."

Laura was standing in front of the mirror, tying and retying her bonnet. "Dr. Mike and Sully are married now. Your life is getting better and better."

Colleen glanced up from her list. "Yes. Laura, you will be careful with the bonnet, won't you? Dr. Mike only wears it on very special occasions."

Laura spun around and smiled. "So do I. And I guess this *is* a special occasion, isn't it?"

Colleen nodded. She touched the straw bonnet she was still wearing. She hoped they wouldn't get into trouble pretending to be each other. She felt awful funny signing the hotel register as Laura McCoy.

Laura flopped on the bed next to Colleen. "We were lucky getting the room with only two beds. Did you hear the man at the desk say that some girls have four to a room?"

"Yes, we're lucky." Colleen took a nervous glance at Dr. Mike's bonnet atop Laura's head. She wished she would take it off soon and hang it on the hook. Dr. Quinn had only loaned it to Colleen, not to a person *pretending* to be Colleen.

Laura was off the bed and leaning out the front window. "You can see all of Main Street from here," she cried. "Do you want to go out and walk around? Maybe we should go to the school and see if we can meet anyone new."

Colleen got up and stood beside Laura. "The

Reverend said we should meet everyone down-stairs at six for supper."

Laura laughed. "Well, the Reverend isn't here now, is he?"

"No, but he is expecting us to follow the rules."

"Colleen, 'A slave to rules is a king of tyrants.' "

"What are you talking about?" asked Colleen.

"Shakespeare," said Laura. "I guess you don't read much Shakespeare at the saloon, do you, Laura?"

"Don't call me Laura," said Colleen. "And I have read some."

Laura sank into a tall rocking chair and grinned. "Just teasing. Listen, we have to get our stories straight. Tell me a few facts about yourself, in case anyone wants to know about me."

"About me?"

"*Me*, silly." Laura was back in front of the mirror, adjusting the curls peeking out from the hat. Suddenly, she frowned. "My dress doesn't go with this fancy bonnet."

Colleen examined the pale blue dress. It was simply made, with white buttons, but very clean and well pressed. "You look fine, Laura."

"Call me *Colleen* or you'll ruin everything."

Colleen sighed. "Listen, I don't know if this is such a good idea. Why don't we just be ourselves, and if you want to pretend that your ma is a doctor, then do it."

Laura crossed her arms. "So, it's all right for me to be you, but you don't want to be saddled with being plain old me, right?"

"That's not what I meant."

Laura turned back to the mirror. "Sure it is. You don't want any of these wonderful people thinking you live above a saloon. You want them to see all your wonderfulness right away."

"It's not like that," began Colleen. "You don't understand."

Laura spun around so fast, the bonnet slipped sideways. "I understand plenty. It's you that lives in some sugar world, not me. Did I tell you that Hank wants me to work for him in a couple of years? He whispered it to me while I was trying to help Ma clean up the kitchen."

"What do you mean?"

"I didn't ask for details," snapped Laura. "Did Hank ever offer you a job? Has Jake Slicker ever had one too many drinks and tried to put his arm around you?" Laura covered her face and started to cry.

"Laura, I . . . " Colleen put her arms around Laura and gave her a hug. "That's so rude and terrible. You're a nice girl, and your grandmother seems awfully nice, too, and . . ."

Laura tried to stop her tears as she shook free from Colleen's hug. "I won't have you feeling sorry for me, you hear?"

"I don't."

Laura turned and slowly took off the fancy satin bonnet. She hung it gently on the hook behind the door. "It was a stupid, silly idea. Why would anyone want to be me, even for a day?"

Colleen felt her own eyes sting, partly from watching Laura crumble into such a sad state, but mostly from shame in knowing she had caused the whole thing.

"Room service!" called a voice above the pounding at the door.

Laura and Colleen both gave each other a puzzled look. Laura shrugged and grabbed a white handkerchief from her pocket, wiping quickly under each eye.

"I'll get it," Colleen said.

Colleen opened the door to face a huge fruit basket wrapped with a curling red, white, and blue ribbon. The basket moved to the left and a handsome young man with bright blue eyes took a step toward her.

"A special basket for a Miss Colleen Cooper. Compliments of Dr. Jack Demos."

Colleen grinned. She remembered Dr. Mike talking about Dr. Demos, a former classmate of her father, Dr. Joseph Quinn.

"Is it all right for me to set it inside?" asked the young man.

Colleen stepped aside and watched as he set the festive basket on the table near the window. Laura still had her back to them.

"Thank you." Colleen glanced down at where her money sock was pinned to her petticoat. It would be too embarrassing to excuse herself and fetch him a coin.

"Well, ladies, have a good day," said the man cheerfully. He took a white tablet from his coat pocket. "Would you mind signing for the basket, please?"

"I . . . " Colleen reached out for the pencil, and then stopped. "Just a second." She looked over at Laura. Her shoulders were hunched, as if she was trying to disappear.

Colleen took the tablet and pencil and turned to Laura, still standing silently by the window. "Colleen, do you want to sign for this, or shall I?"

Laura turned quickly, a smile lighting up her face so totally, she seemed to glow. "Oh, I'd be glad to."

Laura was at the door in a second, scribbling *Colleen Cooper* across the blank sheet so expertly you would have thought she had been doing it all her life.

"Thank you, young man," Laura said politely.

He grinned, allowing two huge dimples to break into his cheeks. "You're welcome, Miss Cooper."

Laura blushed. "Colleen. And this is my good friend, Laura McCoy."

"Wade Loomis," he replied. "My pa said you were here for the big spelling bee, same as me."

"You're the studying son?" blurted out Colleen.

Wade nodded. "I want to win. First prize is ten dollars."

"I didn't even know there was a prize," said Laura.

Colleen laughed. "Maybe the Reverend didn't think we'd win."

Laura joined in the laughing. "Well, may the best man win."

Wade took his tablet and grinned again. "Maybe I should stop studying so much now that I've met my competition."

Laura nodded, then started to close the door. "On the contrary, Mr. Loomis. Now that you've met us, you better study harder than ever."

Before Colleen had time to close her mouth, Laura closed the door on the surprised face of Mr. Wade Loomis.

11

As soon as the door closed, Colleen started to laugh. *"On the contrary?"*

Laura raced across the room and flopped down on the bed. "Oh, my gosh, he is the most beautiful, handsome boy I have ever seen in my life!"

"On the contrary?" repeated Colleen.

Laura sat up and grinned. "I guess that was a bit much, but I was trying to sound like you."

"Me?" sputtered Colleen. "I don't talk like that!"

"I meant it nicely. You don't yell at people," said Laura. "Like me. Even if you get angry. Remember when you found the scarf in your desk?"

Colleen sat up straighter. "I heard you put it there."

Laura cringed, then nodded. "Sorry. I've never had anything so nice. I just had to try it on. I must have had ink on my hands when I picked it up . . ."

66

"You could have gotten me into real trouble, Laura."

Laura nodded again. "I know. I'm sorry. I just got scared and stuck it in your desk. I guess I thought you would discover it right away. I figured you and Alice are friends, so she wouldn't really think you'd ruined it."

Colleen felt better knowing Laura hadn't been trying to get her in trouble. "You could have just admitted you made a mistake."

Laura stared at Colleen. "Oh, sure. And then you would have clapped for me and the Reverend would have given me a big red ribbon for being citizen of the year." Laura got off the bed and started to unpack her bag. "I swear, Colleen. The moment I think I might be able to *talk* to you about something, you turn into this Miss Perfect, and to tell you the truth, it makes me sick."

"I make *you* sick?"

Laura shook out a skirt and refolded it before putting it into the drawer. "Not you, what you say sometimes."

"What I say is who I am!" cried Colleen.

Laura looked over her shoulder and shook her head. "You take yourself *way* too seriously, Colleen."

Colleen scrambled off the bed and unfastened her own suitcase. "Well, maybe that's because I think life is a pretty serious business."

Laura laughed. "You live, you die, and maybe

if you're lucky, you get to have some fun in between."

"That's a terrible way to think about life," said Colleen. She unfolded the jumper Dr. Mike had helped her finish yesterday. It was bright green, with a green plaid vest to match. She shook it out and hung it on the hook in the closet. She took out the white nightgown Dr. Mike had loaned her for the trip and spread it across the narrow twin bed near the wall.

"That's pretty," said Laura softly. She was looking at the nightgown, her arms holding a faded pink gown of her own.

"Dr. Mike has four sisters, so she has lots of fancy nightgowns." Colleen quietly drew in a deep breath. Laura was hard to understand. She could make a person so mad one minute and then say something so nice the next. Laura McCoy was as unpredictable as a colt too wild to be broken, yet wanting somebody to try.

Laura took another sweater and shirt from her carpetbag and then slid it under the bed by the window. "I'm hungry."

Colleen nodded toward her basket. "I still have plenty. Help yourself."

Laura glanced at the basket, then shook her head. "No, Ma said our food came with this trip. I guess I can wait till six."

Colleen walked over and lifted the lid of the basket. "The sandwiches might get spoiled.

Maybe I should pitch them out now. Wouldn't want our room smelling like old cheese."

"Like Mrs. Potts," added Laura. "Oh, okay, maybe I should eat one then, just so we won't smell up the room."

Colleen took one and handed one to Laura. She rolled an orange across the bed. "Better have an orange, too. So Wade Loomis won't see you eating with two forks tonight at supper."

"What?" asked Laura angrily. She tossed the orange from one hand to the other. "Ma taught me how to eat proper."

Colleen sighed. "It was a *joke*, Laura."

Laura stared hard at Colleen, then nodded. "Okay. Thanks."

The two girls ate their sandwiches in silence. As Colleen started to peel her orange, she noticed that Laura was placing hers next to the vase of daisies, and then beside the water pitcher.

"Something wrong with your orange?"

Laura looked up, startled. "No, but Ma sketches a lot, usually while Petey and I study our lessons. She sets potatoes and onions next to pretty things, and next thing you know, she has them turned into an apple or orange in her sketching."

"I wish I could draw well," admitted Colleen. "Can you?"

"Ma's teaching me. I can't make things look real like she can." Laura pointed to Colleen's hat. "She painted that hat for my ma when they lived back East. She had real paints and brushes."

Colleen took the bonnet from her head and studied the flowers. They looked so real you could almost smell them.

Laura set the orange inside her drawer. "I'll take this home to Ma." Laura picked up the rest of her sandwich and sat down on the bed next to Colleen. "It's okay with me if you want to forget about the switch. It was dumb idea."

"It wasn't," insisted Colleen. "I guess I worry about getting in trouble."

Laura nudged Colleen and grinned. "Good reason to be me. I *never* worry about getting in trouble."

Colleen took another bite of her orange, chewing and thinking. For as long as she could remember, she had to worry about staying out of trouble. Once Pa left, and Ma had the whole boardinghouse to run, nobody needed any more trouble to deal with.

"Besides," said Laura, "we'll be home day after tomorrow. I might forget how to be me if I walked too far from it."

Colleen lowered her orange, and tried not to smile. Laura was right. Maybe if she had to be polite, if she had to be nice to people by pretending to be Colleen Cooper, she would realize how easy and pleasant life could be. Dr. Mike and Ma both always said it's not what is in your wallet, but what's in your heart that counts!

Colleen got up and went to the closet. Pulling back the striped cloth, she pulled out her new jumper with the green vest. "We're pretty much the same size, but maybe you better try this on."

Laura looked puzzled this time. "Why?"

"Because Colleen Cooper worries about rules, that's why. And it's a well-known rule that if you're trying to make Wade Loomis crazy about you, your jumper has to fit just so!"

Laura flew off the bed and hugged Colleen. "You mean it? I can be you in Weisport?"

Colleen nodded, feeling excited herself. "Just don't go getting me in trouble."

Laura took the jumper and gave Colleen a stern look. "On the contrary, Miss McCoy, don't you go having so much fun you forget what rules are!"

Both girls started to smile, then laugh. By the time the grandfather clock struck six in the hotel lobby, they had traded both bonnets and identities.

12

That night at supper, Brian's eyes followed Dr. Mike as she moved from stove to table. Every few minutes, she would pop up from the table and offer more food.

"Sit down, Michaela," urged Sully. "We have plenty to eat. You haven't touched your plate."

Dr. Mike smiled nervously and picked up her fork. "Of course I have. Brian, eat your peaches. I heated them with brown sugar, like your mother used to do."

Brian stabbed a peach slice. "I ate four already. And when I got home from school you gave me two apples. I think I'm gonna burst."

Sully laughed.

"I don't see anything funny with wanting Brian to eat properly," said Dr. Mike. She tossed her napkin beside her plate and stood up. "Excuse me, I think I need some fresh air."

Brian took a huge bite of his peach. "Look, Ma. I like this hot peach."

Dr. Mike nodded but hurried outside, hugging her arms against the cool night air. What was wrong with her, anyway? She felt as nervous as a cat on a tin roof.

"You're not worried about Colleen, are you?" Sully came up from behind and wrapped his arms around her waist. "She's safe and looking forward to an adventure."

Dr. Mike leaned back against Sully, feeling safer, yet suddenly, even sadder. His strength belonged to her, protected her, and yet couldn't break through the isolated feeling she had right now. If only she could put her finger on what was worrying her so much. Matthew and Brian were safe inside, seated before platters of food. Colleen was having a wonderful time in Weisport with Laura McCoy, and . . .

Dr. Mike sighed. Laura McCoy. Once the name had been thought, a rush of sadness overcame Dr. Mike with such force, it was as though floodgates had finally been pushed open. The McCoys. A hard-working family living above a saloon that didn't even allow them a healthy diet. With every blink of her eye, Michaela could see blood beneath the fingernails of Maudie McCoy. She had a severe case of scurvy and refused to admit it.

"What were you reading in the clinic?" asked Sully. "It upset you."

"I was reading about scurvy."

Sully turned Dr. Mike to him and grinned.

"Hey, you aren't planning to hop a ship to England are you? I heard scurvy is aboard every ship."

Dr. Mike frowned. "I know. Not too long ago, Englishmen contracted scurvy on plenty of ships."

"So have any landed here in Colorado Springs?" Sully lifted her chin. "What's making you so sad?"

Dr. Mike sighed. "I can't disclose a patient's problem, Sully. Not even to you."

Sully pulled her close. "Well, I'm not a doctor, but I know that someone in town must have scurvy, since it's upsetting you."

Dr. Mike grew serious, pulling away. "You can't mention a word of this, Sully. Promise me."

Sully nodded. "You have my word. Let me know if I can help."

Dr. Mike took his hand and headed back toward the cabin. "Let's go in before we catch pneumonia."

"If we go in, do we have to eat that lime pie you made?"

"It's filled with nutrients," she laughed.

"We're not the ones with scurvy, Michaela. Maybe you should redirect your cooking and baking in another direction."

Dr. Mike pulled him along, smiling. "Stick with me and you'll never have it either."

"Oh, no," laughed Sully. "Maybe not scurvy. I'll just be too large for any horse in Colorado to carry."

As Dr. Mike walked back inside, she kept smiling. Sully was right. All she had to do was to redirect some of the nutritious food to the McCoy family. It would be the simplest prescription she ever had to fill. The hard part would be trying to get Maudie McCoy to accept it.

13

"He's staring at you," whispered Colleen above the rim of her water glass. "He just elbowed the kid with glasses sitting next to him, and now *both* of them are staring at you."

Laura set her fork down and closed her eyes. "I feel sick. I can't do this, Colleen. If they come over here, I swear I will just choke and then die."

"No you won't," insisted Colleen. "Dr. Mike has told you a thousand times to take small bites."

Laura opened her eyes and smiled. "Ma told me the same thing. 'Course, she also told me to check for cigar stubs in the stew."

"What are you two talking about?" asked Lorraine Jones. She was from a town ten miles away and had just sat down at their dining table.

"Hi," Laura said quickly. "I am Colleen Cooper and this is my teammate, Laura McCoy. We are from Colorado Springs."

"Hi. I'm Lorraine. I just got in. Late as usual. My pa insisted on driving me here himself instead of letting me just ride my horse in, like I wanted."

"You wanted to come on a horse?" asked Laura. She raised an eyebrow. "That doesn't sound very safe to me."

Lorraine shook out her napkin. "Well, I help my pa break every horse on our ranch, so riding on a horse seems real safe to me. Truth is, I hate some other fellow steering me. Like in those stagecoaches."

Colleen handed Lorraine the platter of chicken. "Here. It's kind of help yourself."

Lorraine stabbed two pieces of chicken and then stabbed another. "That's the way I like it."

Laura kicked Colleen under the table, but Colleen refused to look at her, afraid she might laugh. Lorraine had scooped up half the mashed potatoes onto her plate and then stuck two biscuits in on each side of the potato mountain.

"Good evening, ladies!"

Colleen jumped as she looked up and into the eyes of Wade Loomis. He was standing next to her elbow, smiling and offering her a dish of mints.

"Would you like some mints, Laura?"

Colleen glanced over at Laura who looked equally surprised. "No, no thank you," Colleen stammered. "But La . . . I mean Colleen and Lorraine might."

Lorraine barely glanced up before she took a handful. She sniffed them and then poured them into her shirt pocket. "Might as well eat these before I turn in. I'm not sure I will be able to get to sleep tonight without the sound of the cattle outside my window."

"Wade, do you know when we're going to meet the judges for the spelling bee?" asked Laura. She shook back her hair and straightened the collar of the dress Colleen had loaned her.

Wade shrugged. "Pa said those fellows are going to walk over right after supper."

Laura stood up quickly. "Well, then. I guess we have time for a quick breath of air. Right, Laura?"

Colleen stood up, then sat down. "Well, I think we'd better wait for Lorraine to finish. I don't want to leave her alone."

Lorraine waved her fork at them all. "Don't worry none about me. I'll be eating till they take the plate."

Wade laughed. "I like to see a girl with a healthy appetite."

Lorraine looked up and grinned. "Don't get too close to me then, fella. My pa says I'm liable to pour gravy on somebody and take a bite of them if I get hungry enough."

Wade laughed again.

"Well, my mother, Dr. Quinn, is always telling me to get my after-dinner air," repeated Laura. She reached down and tugged on Colleen's sleeve. "Don't you remember Ma telling me that, Laura? She told me at the clinic while I was helping stitch up that poor Richard fellow from school. You remember, Laura. That dumb Richard who fell off his horse."

Colleen giggled. "Yes. That dumb Richard. How many stitches did you have to put on that cut?"

"A hundred!" Laura studied her nails. "Took me almost an hour. Plus, he dislocated his shoulder. Popping that back in only took a minute."

"Wow!" said Wade. He set the mints down next to Colleen. "You know how to stitch people and everything?"

Laura nodded, her cheeks growing pinker. "Once I even helped my ma take a bullet out of an Indian chief's neck."

Wade moved closer. "You are really quite a brave girl."

Lorraine reached for another biscuit. "I delivered a calf once. It was stuck so I had to almost crawl inside to get it out. Messy business."

Laura shuddered. "I prefer working with humans, Lorraine."

Colleen passed Lorraine the water. "My ma helped birth a calf once. It's not an easy matter."

Wade shoved his hands in his pockets. "You girls sure are interesting. The girls in Weisport mostly just sew."

Laura laughed, patting her bonnet. "Well, some girls just grow up a little faster."

"I'm near six feet," muttered Lorraine from be-

79

hind her chicken leg. "My sister Mary is six one."

Colleen glanced up at Laura, who was beginning to chew her lower lip. Wade was staring at Lorraine like she was a prized racehorse.

"Wade," said Colleen. "Since your father works at the hotel, maybe you could show . . . Colleen where the fresh air is."

Wade nodded. "Sure." He held out his arm. "Maybe you could tell me some more of your fancy doctor stories. I had an uncle once who just kind of blew up. You ever hear of that? Started off slow, kind of like a bellyache, and then, BOOM. No more Uncle Lenny."

Laura slid her arm through his and looked back over her shoulder at Colleen. "Yes, that sounds like something my mother, the doctor, told me about. I told you about that, right, Laura? The exploding illness?"

Colleen drummed her nails on the table, trying to think. "Oh, yes. I think Ma, I mean your mother called it an appendicitis. Or maybe a burst intestine."

"I love intestine," agreed Lorraine. "Especially with beans."

Laura frowned, looking pale. "Yes, that was it."

As Colleen watched Laura and Wade walk out of the dining room, she started to giggle. She put her napkin in front of her face and tried to stop. Poor Laura. She was probably going to want to give Colleen's bonnet back any minute.

"You feeling all right?" Lorraine asked. She pushed a biscuit closer to Colleen. "You might be having a little gas, Laura. Happens to us all. Eat a biscuit."

Colleen grinned, taking the biscuit and breaking it in two. She leaned back in her chair and studied the other students at their tables. Everyone looked a little nervous. Everyone but Colleen. Why should she be? For the next two days she was Laura McCoy, and she didn't have to answer to anybody.

14

"Where did you gals say you were from?" asked Lorraine. She reached past Colleen and grabbed the gravy. "Boy, this food is good, isn't it?"

"Very good," said Colleen. "Laura . . . I mean, Colleen and I are from Colorado Springs. Have you ever been there?"

Lorraine dipped her biscuit and grinned. "Hey, lady, I tend to stick close to the ranch. Things are so busy I don't have time to shoo the chickens from the kitchen. Only reason I'm wasting time on this spelling bee is the ten dollars. I can use that money to buy a couple of pigs. You like bacon?"

Colleen nodded, glancing over her shoulder. Wade and Laura had been gone a long time. Plenty long enough to get a breath of fresh air. Colleen began to twist her napkin. What if Wade kidnapped Laura? They'd wire Dr. Mike that her daughter was missing, and then all sorts of questions would start flying.

"Well, here we are!" cried Laura. She sat down and sent a smile up at Wade. "See you after the meeting, Wade."

Wade flashed his dimples and went back to his table.

"He's a healthy-looking fella," said Lorraine. "I betcha that boy doesn't have a bad tooth in his whole head."

Laura leaned forward. "He wants to show me something romantic after the meeting."

"He said romantic?" asked Colleen.

"Maybe he meant the moon," offered Lorraine. "That's real romantic, and it's cheap."

Laura shook her head. "I'm sure it's something very special. Wade is very impressed that my mother is a doctor."

Lorraine sat up straighter. "Well, hey. I'm impressed, too, Colleen. It takes a pile of books to digest before you get to be a doctor."

"I'm going to medical school," added Laura. "Back East. I may live with Grandmother Quinn, who lives in a very large house in Boston."

"Gol-ly," said Lorraine. "Hey, there are two girls I met up with before. Linda, Melody, get over here and listen to this girl talk."

Laura blushed. "It's nothing, really."

As soon as Linda and Melody came to the table, Lorraine introduced Laura and Colleen.

"Now, Colleen here is the daughter of a famous doctor who can sew people up and everything," explained Lorraine. "So keep her name on the tip of your tongue in case you end up with food poisoning or something."

Linda sat down at their table. "Actually, my stomach has been very upset all day. I guess it might have been the stage ride, but it keeps on gurgling like some sort of a hot spring."

Colleen leaned forward. "Have you thrown up?"

Linda turned from Laura and frowned at Colleen. "I beg your pardon?"

Colleen blushed. "I was just wondering if you had been sick to your stomach yet?"

"Is your mother a doctor?" Linda asked carefully.

Lorraine shook her head. "No. What did you say your ma does? Sings in the saloon?"

Melody giggled, then covered her mouth with her hand.

"No," corrected Colleen. "My ma is a very fine cook in the saloon kitchen." She sat up straighter. "It's almost like a café."

Laura nodded. "Yes, except Grace owns the café in Colorado Springs. But Laura's ma sure can make a great pot of chili."

"Does she put whiskey in it?" asked Melody, breaking into giggles again.

"Of course not," snapped Colleen. She stood up and looked around the room. "I see Wade's father. I want to ask him when this meeting is going to get started. All of a sudden, I have a terrible headache."

Linda reached out and grabbed Laura's hand. "Hey, maybe the little doc here can give you something for it."

Laura look startled. "Sure. Back in the room."

Colleen crossed her arms. "Okay. Exactly what would you prescribe for my headache, *Colleen*?"

Laura picked up her glass of water and took a long sip. "Well . . ."

Lorraine laughed. "It's just that gas that's bothering you, Laura. Must have settled in your head."

Melody and Linda burst into laughter. Laura choked on her water, and Lorraine looked confused.

"I didn't mean nothing by that," stammered Lorraine.

Colleen reached down and patted Lorraine as she hurried past. "I know you didn't, Lorraine."

Colleen was just about to rush up to Mr. Loomis and ask when the meeting was about to start when a tall man with a red-whiskered beard called the students to order.

15

"My name is Richard Easton, and I am fortunate enough to be the teacher here in Weisport. First of all, let me welcome each and every one of you to the spelling competition." He took out a hanky and wiped his forehead. "I hope you liked your supper. Maybe we could give a little hand for the nice people at the Copeland Hotel for their nice service."

Colleen slid into a free chair and clapped. She leaned backwards and saw Laura, still busy chatting with three more new girls at the table. Laura was acting like the entire supper had been scheduled to welcome her to Weisport. Nobody seemed to notice that Colleen had even left the table.

"Hey, what are you doing over here by yourself?" whispered Wade.

Colleen jumped, then put a finger in front of her lips. All she needed now was to have Mr. Easton stop the meeting so he could shush Colleen.

Wade sank into a chair, pulling it up close to Colleen. "Having any fun so far? Not much going on in this town. Bored?"

Colleen shook her head, then directed her attention back to Mr. Easton.

"And the spelling bee will kick off tomorrow at nine o'clock at the school. Refreshments will be served from nine to nine-thirty, giving us a little bit more time to welcome our guests. Then, round one will begin. I'm afraid that we will move rather quickly with the spelling bee, giving each student only one chance to spell a word correctly. Once you miss a word, you must sit down."

A groan went up from the students.

Mr. Easton chuckled and held up both hands. "You can sit down and enjoy the refreshments and cheer on the other members of your team. Now, it's almost eight o'clock, so I suggest that you all return to your hotel rooms and get a good night's sleep. There is still time for a good hour of studying those spelling words, as well. Good night and good luck to you all!"

Colleen smiled and clapped hard. Mr. Easton seemed like a really nice man. And it seemed like a really good idea to go upstairs and study her words. Ma and the boys would be so proud of her if she brought home a trophy.

Wade tugged on Colleen's hair. "Let's get out of here."

Colleen almost laughed. Was Wade offering tours for all the visiting girls?

"I think I'd better get La . . . I mean Colleen, and head upstairs. We should study our spelling list."

Wade shook his head and grinned. "And here I was thinkin' that you were going to bring a little fun into town."

Colleen glanced around the room. The students were all standing now, talking and laughing as they moved around the room. Everyone seemed to be having fun already.

"Is something planned for tonight?" she asked. Maybe Mr. Easton had mentioned a social to follow the meeting.

Wade stood up and took Colleen's arm. "I asked Colleen to meet me outside at nine, but she said she didn't want to get in trouble breaking any rules."

"That's true. Reverend Johnson is counting on us to follow the rules," admitted Colleen quickly. "Right down to the last little rule."

Wade leaned closer. "Well, seems to me that you might have your own set of rules, Laura. Am I right?"

Colleen jerked away. "No."

Wade laughed. "Don't tell me your ma makes you study hard every night like my pa does me. He keeps telling me to study hard or I'll never see the inside of a college."

"My ma tells me the same. I want to be a doctor."

Wade's eyebrows shot up. "A doctor? Maybe specializing in firewater, huh? What kind of wages does a saloon cook get to send her girl off to medical school?"

Colleen stood up fast, slapping Wade hard on his arm. "Be quiet. My ma values education, same as your pa does."

As Wade got up, he glared at Colleen. "What is this, some little church girl act? We have saloons in Weisport, too, you know."

"So?"

"So, don't go pretending that you want to study hard and go to medical school. You'll be lucky if you finish grammar school. No telling when your ma might need some help in the kitchen."

Colleen felt a fuse being lit inside her. Her cheeks flushed red, and without taking another second to think about it, she reached for a glass of water and splashed it in Wade's face!

"Children!" gasped Mr. Easton. He rushed forward and handed Wade his handkerchief. "What is going on?"

"I don't know," cried Wade from behind the handkerchief.

"I don't either!" cried Colleen. She reached out, shook Mr. Easton's hand, and ran out of the dining room.

16

"Are you crazy?" cried Laura. She closed the hotel door and shook her head. "I swear, Colleen. Half the town is talking 'bout you hitting Wade Loomis!"

Colleen covered her face. "I didn't *hit* him. He got a little wet is all. He's horrid, Laura. You're a fool if you ever talk to him again."

"A fool?" Laura closed her eyes and waltzed around the room. "He is the most handsome, romantic boy I have ever met. He thinks I'm wonderful."

"He tried to get me to leave the hotel with him." Colleen shuddered. "He said he figured I was bored."

Laura laughed. "Well, he was just trying to make you feel at home."

"He was acting like Jake Slicker, if you want to know the truth," said Colleen.

Laura's smile froze. "Oh, no. You mean 'cause your ma works in the saloon?"

"*Your* ma, Laura." Colleen reached around and started to unsnap her dress. "I am getting out of your dress and into *my* nightgown so I can study my words and get to sleep."

Laura hurried over and cradled Colleen's fancy nightgown to her cheek. "Oh, Colleen. You said I could wear it, please? We'll be on the stage day after tomorrow. Please don't ruin things."

Colleen sighed, then grabbed Laura's nightgown. "Well, all right, but don't leave me alone with Wade again. If he makes one more crack to me, I'm going to crack him."

Laura giggled. "Now, would the old Colleen be talking this way?"

Colleen slipped the nightgown over her head, glad her face was hidden. The old Colleen would be having the fun that Laura was busy having.

Laura lifted the shade and peered outside. "It's dark. I guess Dr. Quinn's daughter wouldn't be allowed to walk alone at this time of night, would she?"

"Dr. Quinn's daughter would be studying her spelling words," mumbled Colleen as she grabbed her list and climbed under the covers. "I plan to beat Wade Loomis tomorrow."

Laura went to the closet and examined Colleen's dresses. "Too bad you didn't bring your new rose dress. I would have looked great in that."

Colleen rolled her eyes, then went back to her list. "Subscribe, S-U-B-S-C-R-I-B-E."

91

Laura sat on the edge of the bed and gently lowered the list. "Favor, F-A-V-O-R."

What are you talking about?"

"Colleen, I know you want to study, but I have a very important favor to ask."

"All right, I will not strangle Wade Loomis tomorrow."

Laura laughed. "Thanks. But, I was wondering if you could fix my hair like you did yours for the Valentine dance? With the braids on the side? You looked so pretty. Petey came home and said you were the prettiest girl he ever saw."

Colleen smiled. "He did?"

Laura hopped off the bed, returning with a brush. The handle was beautifully carved with wild flowers. "Please?"

Colleen examined the brush. "This is lovely. How did it get cracked?"

Laura sighed. "It was my mother's. I dropped it, or rather, threw it, when I found out I had to go live with Ma at the saloon. Wish I had kept my temper in."

The two girls stared at the brush, silent as they remembered all the things that couldn't be mended.

Colleen picked up a hank of Laura's thick blond hair and ran the brush through it. "Retaliate. Spell."

"R-E-T-A-L-I-A-T-E." Laura spelled quickly. "Now yours. Onion sandwich."

Colleen laughed. "O-N-I-O-N S-A-N-D-W-I-C-H. Okay, ink stain." She stopped brushing. "Sorry."

Laura shook her head. "I have done some pretty stupid things since I came to Colorado Springs."

Colleen saw the sadness growing in Laura's green eyes. "Hey, forget that. How about . . . Loomis, as in Wade."

Laura's face brightened immediately. "L-O-O-M-I-S!"

Colleen handed Laura the braid. "Hold this while I find a ribbon."

As Colleen rummaged through her basket, Laura got off the bed and carefully tiptoed to stand in front of the mirror. "I look pretty, like you, Colleen."

Colleen pulled out two green ribbons and stood behind Laura. "You are pretty, Laura, like yourself. Especially when you smile."

Laura shrugged. "Pretending to be Dr. Quinn's daughter gives me more to smile about, I guess."

Colleen sighed. "Your grandmother is very well liked in town, Laura. Give her a chance."

Laura nodded. "I know. It's just been so hard lately. All she does is snap at Petey and me. And something's wrong with her, I just know it. She has purple bruises all over." Laura turned and sat down in the rocking chair, her braid slipping out of the ribbon. "Don't tell anybody, Colleen. Ma said people would take Petey and me away and lock us up in an orphanage if they thought she was sick."

Colleen knelt down beside the chair. "Dr. Mike could help her. She knows so much about most everything. I could ask her to . . ."

Laura looked up, her face stricken. "Promise me, Colleen. Nobody is going to split Petey and me up. I'll run away if they try. Soon as I'm old enough, I'm going to get married and take Petey. Ma doesn't want us. Nobody wants us."

"Laura . . . " Colleen stopped, running her fingers under her own eyes. "That's silly."

"You crying?"

Colleen nodded, looking up and trying to smile. "It's my life you're talking about, lady."

Laura giggled, then started to laugh. "Wow, look at us. I think we've both gone nuts."

Colleen stood up and pulled Laura up. "Come on, let's work on these braids. Maybe if you look so absolutely beautiful, Wade will be so mesmerized, he will misspell his word."

Laura nodded. "M-E-S-M-E-R-I-Z-E-D."

Colleen finished the second braid and stood back, admiring her work. "Ravishing. R-A-V-I-S-H-I-N-G."

Laura turned and curtseyed. "T-H-A-N-K-S."

"Get changed and let's study," suggested Colleen. "Reverend took our stage funds out of the collection basket. I think he's counting on us coming back with the trophy."

"Okay," agreed Laura. "Don't worry, Colleen. I just know we won't be coming back to Colorado Springs empty-handed."

17

Dr. Mike walked slowly up the alley leading to Mrs. McCoy's kitchen. She balanced her medical bag in one hand and a basket of oranges, apples, and tomatoes in the other. When she reached the door, she tapped several times with the tip of her shoe. "Mrs. McCoy?"

Dr. Mike waited, then tapped again. "Maudie? It's me, Dr. Mike. Can I come in?"

Still not hearing anything, Dr. Mike set down her medical bag and carefully opened the door. "I received a shipment of oranges today, and I . . ."

Dr. Mike stepped into the kitchen. Maudie McCoy was slumped across the kitchen table, while a kettle boiled over on the stove, black smoke pouring from beneath the lid.

Dr. Mike set the basket down on the table, rushing over to grab the pot off the burner with a thick towel.

"Ohhhh!" she cried, clattering the scalding pot

down with such force it toppled over and rolled crazily across the floor.

Maudie jerked up, wiping the corner of her mouth as she stood up and grabbed the broom. "Stand back," she cried, trying to pick the smoldering pot up by the wired handle.

"Be careful," Dr. Mike called, stepping back as sparks flew from the stove. Dr. Mike turned and threw a pitcher of water on the stove, sending up more black smoke.

"What's going on in there?" shouted Hank from the other room.

"Nothing," Maudie called back. "Fixin' supper, Hank."

Maudie carried the smoldering pot out the kitchen door and hurried back in, mopping the floor with rags stuffed in both hands. "Don't let him come in here, Dr. Mike. Second time this week I fell asleep while the stove was lit. He'll fire me for sure."

Dr. Mike opened the window and fanned out the black smoke.

"You trying to burn my place down, Maudie?" hollered Hank. His angry voice was getting closer and closer to the door.

"It's . . . fine," stammered Maudie. She glanced up at Dr. Mike from the floor, two sorrowful eyes circled with dark smudges.

With a quick glance at the door, Dr. Mike

grabbed her shawl and shoved it down the stove burner, hopping back as it caught fire and began to shrivel.

Hank flew into the room. "What are you fool women up to now?" He grabbed a bucket of soapy water and threw it on the stove.

"It's all my fault," cried Dr. Mike. "I stood too close to the burner and my shawl caught fire." Dr. Mike tried to catch Maudie's eye. "If Mrs. McCoy hadn't been so quick, I might have been badly burned."

Hank stared at Dr. Mike, then glared at Maudie. "This woman ain't been quick about anything for the past two months. Now clean this place up!"

Hank slammed the door on his way out.

Dr. Mike picked up her shawl and dropped it into the tub by the window. "I'll help you."

Maudie got wearily to her feet, dropping her rags into the tub as well. "You already have, Dr. Mike. I feel real bad about your shawl and making you lie."

Dr. Mike glanced at the door. "Hank wasn't in the mood for the truth."

Maudie stared down into the tub. "I don't know when I can replace that shawl for you."

Dr. Mike put her hand on Maudie's shoulder. "Your health is more important than the shawl, Maudie."

Maudie shook off her hand. "I'm fine. Been

working too hard lately. I've been trying to make Petey some new trousers for school and . . ."

"Unless your scurvy is treated, you'll get progressively more tired," explained Dr. Mike. "You can't ignore it, Maudie. Unless treated, scurvy can lead to death."

Maudie's head jerked up. "No. British soldiers got it on ships traveling to America. They weren't dead when they got here."

"They started eating limes and tomatoes. They recovered, and so can you."

Maudie sank into the chair. "I got to take care of those two kids. Although all I do is bark at them. Poor kids. Their daddy left, ma died, and they end up with the mean old kitchen witch."

Dr. Mike picked up her medical bag. "Irritability is a very common symptom, Maudie. It's your body telling you to get help."

Maudie jerked her head toward the door. "Hank must have a worse case of scurvy than I do, then."

Dr. Mike laughed and opened her bag. "I want to give you some medicine to get you started. I brought some fruit, and a few packages of tomato seeds to grow your own, and . . ."

Maudie stood up. "I'm not taking charity. I'll start trying to get some vegetables on my own."

Dr. Mike sighed. "I'm a doctor. This isn't charity."

Maudie shook her head. "I appreciate the offer, but I've always worked hard and paid my own way." She hesitated. "Here, take this. Maybe you can find a place for it."

From beside the shelves, Maudie lifted a picture of wildflowers in a rickety wooden frame. "It's not much of a frame, but the flowers are pretty."

Dr. Mike examined the charcoal sketch. The flowers were so lifelike, they seemed to wave in the breeze.

"Oh, Maudie. This is lovely. Did it belong to your family?"

Maudie ducked her head, blushing. "I did it myself. Used the stove coals."

Dr. Mike smiled. "I love it. I'll hang it in the clinic this very afternoon."

Dr. Mike got out a packet and poured some powder in a glass. "I want you to drink this, and eat at least two oranges a day until further notice."

"I don't know."

"You aren't trying to back out of our agreement, are you?" Dr. Mike crossed her arms and tried to look stern.

Maudie grinned. "Okay, the fruit for the drawing." Maudie took the broom and shook her head at the mess. "I better get started in here."

"Let me help," offered Dr. Mike.

"No thanks," laughed Maudie. "I appreciate the offer, Dr. Mike, but I don't think the kitchen is a real safe place for you."

Dr. Mike laughed. As she walked past the table,

she rolled an apple toward Maudie. "Eat while you sweep."

Maudie caught the apple and smiled back. "I thank you for your help, Dr. Mike."

"Call me Michaela," Dr. Mike said cheerfully. "And that's what neighbors are for."

As Dr. Mike left Maudie McCoy's kitchen, she began to smile. With the warmth she suddenly felt inside, she wondered if she would ever need a shawl again.

18

Pounding on the hotel door awakened Colleen and Laura. The doorknob rattled, and finally Lorraine called through the crack beneath the door.

"Hey, you two sleepyheads. Wake up! You missed a real good breakfast, and Mr. Easton is about to cart us all over to the school for the spelling bee!"

"Oh, my gosh!" cried Colleen, tumbling out of bed and falling to the floor in a tangled knot of bedsheets.

"We fell back to sleep!" cried Laura. She grabbed the end of the bedspread and wrapped it around herself before she flung open the door.

Lorraine's eyes grew wide. "Holy cow. You girls sure can mess up a room. They should have put you both in the barn."

"Tell Mr. Easton we'll be right down," called Colleen from the floor. "Don't let them start the spelling bee without us."

Lorraine nodded, pulling the door closed. "Okay. I'll see if I can rustle up some bread and jam for you both, too."

"Thanks, Lorraine," Laura called as the door shut.

Both girls flew into their clothes, helping each other button and braid.

"My hair looks terrible!" whined Laura. "I looked so nice last night."

Colleen retied Laura's ribbon. "It's the best I can do. Now hurry up."

"Wade will wonder what happened to me overnight," muttered Laura as she slid her foot into Colleen's shoe. "I wish you wore my size."

Colleen reached over and snatched back her shoe. "Absolutely not. I refuse to give you my shoes."

Laura grinned. "Okay. Let's go. We spent too much time talking last night."

"You were the one who suddenly wanted to tell me about every friend you ever made," Colleen insisted. She grabbed her brush and yanked it through her hair.

The doorknob jiggled again. "Everyone is on the porch," called Lorraine. "Come on!"

The three girls pounded down the stairs and outside. Lorraine slipped each of them a biscuit.

"Are we all here?" Mr. Easton asked. He checked his list and counted heads. "Get aboard and let the spelling bee begin."

"I was beginning to think you weren't coming," said Wade. He lifted Laura by the waist onto the wagon. He turned and offered Colleen a lift, but she swatted his hands away and allowed Mr. Easton to help her. Lorraine hitched up one side of her skirt and hopped aboard herself.

Wade seated himself next to Laura. He picked up a piece of straw and tickled her neck. "There's a celebration dance after the spelling bee ends. Want to go with me?"

Laura looked over at Colleen. Colleen rolled her eyes but didn't say a word.

"That sounds real nice, Wade. I'd love to go."

"I'm not much of a dancer myself," confided Lorraine. She wedged herself in between Wade and Laura. "I never could get my feet going proper. But I sure do like to play the fiddle. You think somebody might loan me one, Wade?"

Wade nodded. "My pa fiddles."

Lorraine slapped her leg. "Well, there you go then." She leaned over and tapped Colleen. "How's the stomach feeling today?"

Colleen choked on her biscuit, her cheeks burning. If Lorraine *dared* to mention gas, she would jump right under the wagon wheels.

"Okay, here we are!" called out Mr. Easton from the front wagon.

The Weisport schoolhouse was beautiful, with a large bell tower. It was still only one large room, but the tall windows on either side let in lots of sunlight. Carriages and wagons were already scattered along the yard, with adults standing in groups, sipping lemonade and eating cookies.

"This looks like a real party," said Colleen.

Wade nodded, then tugged on her sleeve. "Maybe a little tame for you, Laura."

Colleen elbowed past him as she was helped off the wagon. "Wade Loomis, you are the most vile person I have ever encountered."

Wade and his friends hooted.

"Vile?" questioned Wade. "Care to spell that?"

Laura stood up and turned to Wade. "You be nice to my good friend, Wade Loomis, or you can find yourself another partner for the dance tonight."

"You better play nice," advised one boy.

Colleen glared at them all and followed the others across the yard. Had she been blind to the treatment Laura had endured in Colorado Springs, or was Wade Loomis just a rotten kid?

Colleen and Laura were still so hungry that they ate six cookies apiece. They were on their third glass of lemonade when the school bell started to clang.

"It's time," whispered Colleen. "Remember, say the word first, then divide it in your head and spell it."

"Okay." Laura dusted the cookie crumbs from her mouth and brushed off her skirt. She grinned at Colleen. "Thanks for letting me wear this."

Colleen brushed off the pale green skirt she was wearing. "Thanks for letting me wear this."

Laura stiffened. "You joking me?"

Colleen shook her head quickly. "No, no, I mean it. I like this skirt, and . . ." Colleen swallowed hard, praying the words would come out right. "And I hope that if anyone is ever unfair to you, La . . . Colleen, I hope I'll be there to stick up for you. Same as you did for me with Wade."

Laura yanked gently on Colleen's braid. "Trust me. I never walk away from a fight."

"Girls!" called Mr. Easton from the school steps. "We have been waiting on you two all morning."

Colleen and Laura grabbed their skirts and ran across the yard. In less than five minutes, the spelling bee would begin. The waiting was over!

19

"*Knowledgeable*," stated Mr. Easton.

Colleen kept smiling straight ahead, but let her eyes dart to the right. A pretty girl with two dozen freckles dancing across her face began to spell.

"Correct." Mr. Easton smiled broadly out at the audience as if he had spelled the word himself. "The second word is: *ricochet*."

Colleen forgot to smile and gulped. She felt Laura tug on her skirt. Neither one of them would want that word.

Three students went down on ricochet. Colleen groaned as Wade spelled it properly. His parents clapped loudly from the front row.

"Now, we are proud that our hometown boy got such a difficult word," expressed Mr. Easton. "I'm afraid the next word is a tricky one as well. *Reconcile*."

Colleen and Laura both cleared their throats at the same time. Colleen bit the inside of her lip so

107

she wouldn't laugh. So much had happened in such a short time. Laura and Colleen had gone from *retaliate* to *reconcile* to friends.

For the next twenty minutes words flew up and down the spelling line. Four spellers, including Wade, sat down for misspelling *idiom*. Wade insisted that he said D, not T, but Mr. Easton told him to sit down anyway. Colleen was glad to see him slink off the stage. He was truly a nice-looking young man, but his manners were so offensive, they canceled out his dark eyelashes and dimples. On the stage ride home, Colleen was going to have to have a long talk with Laura. Even Richard was nicer than Wade Loomis! In fact, if . . .

"Miss McCoy?" Mr. Easton was standing in front of her, his face a feather distance away from her own. "Can you please spell the word."

Colleen felt faint. "The word?"

"*Systematize,*" Mr. Easton said slowly. He bit off each syllable so sharply, Colleen could smell his breakfast bacon.

"*Systematize,*" repeated Colleen. "S-Y-S-T-E-M-A-T-I-Z-E!"

"Correct!" cried Laura.

Mr. Easton lowered his spectacles and studied Laura. "All right now, the next word is: *ridicule.*"

Colleen could hear Laura inhale.

"*Ridicule,*" repeated Laura softly. "R-I-D-A . . . Sorry, I wish to start again."

"You may," replied Mr. Easton.

"*Ridicule*," Laura began. "R-I-D-I-C-U-L."

A slight murmur arose from the audience.

"I'm sorry," said Mr. Easton, extending a small, sympathetic frown. "I shall have to ask you to sit down and offer the same word to our guest who is here all the way from Castle Rock."

Colleen reached out and caught Laura's hand as she left the stage. Inside, Colleen's heart began to pound. The word *ridicule* had been on the spelling list. If only they had studied the words more last night. Reverend Johnson would be upset when he heard the word Laura misspelled. He would be even more unsettled if Colleen missed a word from the list as well.

Laura took a seat next to Wade. Even though Colleen couldn't stand Wade Loomis, she was glad to see Wade smile and reach out to shake Laura's hand. What worried Colleen more was Laura's yanking the fancy satin bonnet from her head and leaving it on the chair beside her. Colleen worried that the next disappointed student to leave the stage would sit on it.

"Miss McCoy?"

Colleen jumped, looking first at Laura sitting in the audience. Laura pointed toward Mr. Easton.

Colleen looked to the right, surprised that she was one of only four students left on the stage.

"Would you please spell *sanctimoniousness*?" Even Mr. Easton glanced back down at his list.

"Take your time, Miss. The words are getting rather hard, aren't they?"

"I . . . " Colleen closed her eyes. Had that word been on the list? She knew it meant something about lying, or being a hypocrite. Colleen coughed, hoping her heart wouldn't fly right out of her mouth. Suddenly, she remembered! Reverend Johnson had put the word on the chalkboard, circling vowel after vowel to illustrate how tricky some words at the spelling bee could get. Yes, he had circled, five, no, no, seven vowels! Colleen tried to picture the circles in her mind.

With her eyes still closed tightly, Colleen began: "*Sanctimoniousness.* S-A-N-C-T-I-M-O-N-I-O-U-S-N-E-S-S!" Colleen finished with a soft hiss.

The audience clapped and Colleen opened her eyes.

"Very good," congratulated Mr. Easton. "The next word is *nonsensical.*"

Colleen was so relieved to be finished with her word, she wasn't even upset that the next few words seemed easy. She kept telling herself that the only reason she was having such a hard time was because she had been up half the night talking to Laura.

Five minutes later, Colleen was one of three students left on stage. She was sandwiched between Lorraine and a boy named Carl from Castle Rock.

Lorraine spelled *despitefulness* correctly. Colleen stammered her way through *malicious*, and Carl went to his seat after misspelling *reiterate*.

Mr. Easton flipped to the last page of his spelling words. Colleen was so nervous she almost yelped when Lorraine gave her hand a hearty squeeze. Colleen gave Lorraine a faint squeeze back and gave Laura a weary smile. The afternoon sun was blazing through all twelve windows. Colleen felt warmer than a baked apple standing on stage. Sweat trickled from beneath her straw hat, rolling slowly down the back of her neck. She watched as Lorraine quickly spelled *ingression*.

"Good job," whispered Colleen as the audience clapped. Lorraine was smart. Smart to have spelled a word of which Colleen had never even heard, and smart to have worn a short-sleeved shirt and a skirt. Her hair was tied back with a thin piece of rawhide.

Mr. Easton rustled his papers and beamed at the audience. "I wish to thank and congratulate all twenty-four students who participated in the first annual Weisport spelling bee. Let's give them all a nice round of applause."

When the clapping subsided, Mr. Easton cleared his throat. "Now, for the task at hand. I will give Miss McCoy and Miss Jones each another word. Within the next five minutes, we will have our champion, who will proudly carry the trophy home. In addition, the champion will be invited to return and present the trophy to next year's champion.

"Miss McCoy, please spell *paralysis*."

Laura covered her face. Wade smirked. Lorraine leaned over and gave her an encouraging smile.

Colleen grinned. She never saw the word on the Reverend's spelling list, but she had seen it plenty of times in Dr. Mike's medical books.

"*Paralysis*," Colleen said cheerfully. "P-A-R-A-L-I-S-I-S."

Laura uncovered her face and grinned at Colleen. Wade looked disappointed. Colleen beamed, waiting for Lorraine's word.

"I'm sorry," said Mr. Easton, his finger still on the spelling list. "I will ask Miss Jones to spell the same word. If she is successful, she is our winner."

"What?" Colleen blurted out. Hadn't she spelled it correctly?

Lorraine licked her lips and began slowly. "*Paralysis*. P-A-R-A-L-Y-S-I-S!"

The audience began clapping before Mr. Easton could reach out his hand to shake Lorraine's. Colleen groaned. She couldn't even remember if she had said Y or I.

Lorraine slapped Colleen on the back. "You did real well, Laura." She leaned closer and lowered her voice. "Especially with standing up here for hours with your little problem."

Colleen stared back, wondering if Lorraine meant her stomach pains or switched identity.

Laura raced on stage, hugging Colleen. "You came in second. That's wonderful."

Colleen shrugged. "Second doesn't come with a trophy. Looks like we're going to head back tomorrow morning empty-handed."

"Who cares," laughed Laura, pulling Colleen toward the stage steps. "The good news is that Wade has found a fella for you for the dance tonight."

"What?" Colleen glanced nervously in Wade's direction. He was busy laughing with two other boys. The nice boy named Carl from Castle Rock shook his head and walked away. A large, older-looking boy with a neck the size of an oak tree began to nod his head and grin. He looked up and smiled at Colleen. From a distance, he looked as if he were growing a mustache. Colleen's smile froze. The young man raised one huge hand and waved.

"I'm not going," whispered Colleen. "That boy looks older than Sully."

"He's only fourteen. Come on, it will be fun," Laura whispered back. "Please? It's our last night of being each other. I promise we'll stick together the whole time. Come on, Colleen. You're Laura. I *always* choose a good time."

Colleen stared back at the boy. He spit on a hanky and wiped off a stain from his vest. Colleen felt terrible judging him. If she had learned one thing at Weisport, it was not to judge someone by their appearance or by what their parents did for a living. What choice did a newborn baby have in all that?

"Okay," Colleen said at last. "I'll go. But we stick together, okay? And if it gets too awful, we say good night and go upstairs to pack."

"Great. I'll give Wade the good news."

As Laura broke through the crowd to Wade, Colleen tried not to worry. She took off her bonnet and shook back her hair. When Wade glared at her across the room, she forced herself to smile and wave back as if he were a nice boy. Laura was right. This was their last night in Weisport. The dance might be the perfect ending to their adventure. In fewer than twenty-four hours, she would be on the stage heading back to Colorado Springs. What could possibly happen?

20

"I like the picture, Ma." Brian set down the hammer. "How did I do with hanging it?"

Dr. Mike straightened the picture and took a step back. "Sully will probably want you to start helping him around the house, Brian."

Brian whooped around the clinic. "That would be so much fun. You know what else would be real fun, Ma?"

"What's that, Brian?"

"If Mrs. McCoy could come to the school sometime and teach us how to draw so good."

"She draws *well*," corrected Dr. Mike.

Brian nodded. "I think so, too."

"Well, I'm going to see Mrs. McCoy tomorrow afternoon, Brian. I'll ask her about that. I think it's a wonderful idea."

"Tell Reverend we don't need so much time on history," suggested Brian. "Tell him Mrs. McCoy can teach us to draw pictures of George Washington, instead of learning so much about him cutting down some dumb tree."

"Brian," laughed Dr. Mike. "Reverend Johnson was trying to teach you how honest George Washington was. He cut down the tree, and when asked, he admitted he did it."

Brian shook his head. "Sounds kind of dumb to me, Ma."

"I hope that you are brave enough to tell the truth, Brian."

"All the time?"

"Yes. Truth isn't something you use now and then like some sort of pocket watch."

Brian put the hammer back in his toolbox. "Don't you ever want to lie?"

Dr. Mike blushed, remembering the shawl she shoved into Maudie's stove. "Yes. And sometimes I tell a lie. But it's never something I'm proud of. It's something I do in a panic, when I'm afraid of what the truth might cause."

"What does that mean?"

Dr. Mike smiled. "It means I feel so much better when I can tell the truth, Brian. I feel fresher, cleaner. Like you do when you've spent the afternoon playing outside in the bright sunlight with Wolf."

Brian grinned. "Oh, I get it now."

Dr. Mike picked up her medical bag. "Ready to go home for supper?"

Brian stopped, then shrugged. "What are we having?"

"Stew. Same as last night. But I'm going to try to make some biscuits. And nobody has touched my lime pie."

"Oh."

"Hungry?"

Brian nodded, then shook his head. "You like the truth, don't you Ma?"

"Of course I do, Brian."

"Well, then I guess I'm a little hungry. But, if you want my sunshine answer, your stew ain't so good."

Dr. Mike tried not to frown. "My stew *isn't* so good."

Brian smiled and took Dr. Mike's hand. "That's okay, Ma. Colleen will be back soon."

Dr. Mike smiled and laughed. "I can hardly wait till Colleen comes home, myself."

21

"I just dread going home tomorrow to tell Dr. Mike the bad news," said Colleen. She walked over to Laura and turned around. "Would you mind helping me with these buttons?"

Laura set her brush down. "Are you sure you don't mind wearing my dress? It isn't nearly as pretty as the one I get to wear."

Colleen shook her head. "I think this is real pretty. And your grandmother is so artistic. How did she get these pumpkin seeds to stick on the collar?"

Laura laughed. "Some sort of saddle glue she got from Robert E at the livery stable. She soaked them all night in blueberry juice, to turn them that nice color."

"You sound proud of her, Laura. You must love her some."

Laura finished buttoning the rest of the dress in silence. Finally, she answered. "I guess she's easier to love when I'm here in Weisport being you. I can't hear her yelling at me and complaining that Petey and I don't treat her sweet enough."

Colleen turned around and grabbed Laura's hand. "You weren't so sweet to anyone back home, Laura."

Laura took her hand away. "How sweet would you feel, having someone fuss at you over breakfast?"

"All I'm saying is, if it takes a pretty dress to make you feel happy, then take mine," said Colleen. "Keep them, I don't care."

Laura looked surprised. "You mean it?"

"I do. I think once you wear them and treat people nice, then they'll be nice right back. Pretty soon, you'll know that you can wear anything and people will still like you."

Laura's smile shrank, then disappeared. "How can you say that? You've seen how people treat you here, Colleen? That's what I get all the time."

"Wade's the only one who has been rude."

"What about the girls at supper the other night? Melody and Linda. They asked you if your ma put whiskey in the stew."

"I know. And it made me mad. But maybe I should have just laughed, or told them what a good cook my ma is. Just 'cause they were rude, doesn't mean I have to be rude right back."

Laura picked up the hairbrush and began to comb out the braids Colleen had just put in her hair. "I guess it's real easy to be perfect for a couple of days, isn't it, Colleen? Like being brave when you get stitches 'cause you know it will be over soon and you won't have to walk around with a needle in your arm for the rest of your life."

"Oh, phooey!" sputtered Colleen. She took the brush from Laura's hand and set it down with a bang. "That's a lot of crybaby talk. Nobody's making you wake up every morning and stick that needle back in your arm but you, Laura."

Laura glared at Colleen, then quietly picked up the brush. "I can hardly wait to go back home tomorrow. I can hardly wait for you to leave me alone."

"Me, too," snapped Colleen. "I'll be glad to have a *real* friend like Becky."

Colleen walked to the door. She glanced at the bonnets hanging side by side. She reached up and touched the soft satin of Dr. Mike's, then ran her fingers along the rough, hand-painted flowers of Laura's.

"Which one will you be wearing tonight, Colleen?" Laura didn't sound mad anymore, just tired.

"It's too late in the evening for a bonnet," Colleen said softly. "I won't be wearing either to the dance."

22

The dining room of the hotel had been decorated for the dance. Streamers hung from the rafters and all the tables had been pushed to one side.

Colleen searched the room for a friendly face. Maybe she should go back upstairs and wait for Laura. She certainly didn't want to entertain Wade and his large friend by herself.

"Hey, how are you?" Lorraine grinned, lifting a small plate piled high with fudge squares. "I figure I better celebrate tonight. Tomorrow I'm going to go back early and buy me some pigs with my ten dollars."

"Too bad the stages weren't running tonight," said Colleen. Suddenly she felt very homesick. She missed having a best friend around like Becky, someone who was always careful about not hurting people's feelings.

"Oh, no," whispered Lorraine. "There you go again with that look. You having some more gas?"

"No!" sputtered Colleen. "Please stop talking about . . ."

Lorraine took a big bite of a fudge square. "All part of life as far as I can make out." Lorraine took another bite and handed Colleen her plate. "Mind watching this for me? I see Mr. Loomis over there with his fiddle. I want to see if I can play a little tonight. I bet your friend Colleen will get lots of dances. She sure is friendly, ain't she?"

Colleen nodded, then took the plate and looked around for a dark corner to hide in. Once Laura left the room, Colleen was planning to go back upstairs and lie down. She wasn't in the mood for pretending anymore.

"Well, hey!"

Colleen looked up, and up still further. Wade's friend was standing in front of her. He was wearing a clean vest and smelled like lye soap.

"I'm Wade's friend, Billy. You're Laura. I remember you from this afternoon. You did a good job with those words."

"Thank you, Billy." Colleen offered him Lorraine's plate of fudge squares. "Would you like one?"

Billy reached out and took five. "Sure thing. Wade will be here directly."

"So will La . . . Colleen."

"Where are you girls from again?" asked Billy.

"Colorado Springs."

Billy put two fudge squares in his mouth. He chewed quietly, smiling at Colleen. When he finished the last fudge square, he got out a handkerchief and wiped off his hands. "I don't want to get you all smeared once the dancing starts."

"Thank you." Colleen glanced toward the stairs. If only Laura would come down now, she could make a hasty exit upstairs before the dancing *could* start.

"Do your folks mine or farm?" asked Billy.

"I live with my grandmother," Colleen said slowly. She drew in a deep breath, wondering if Wade had already filled Billy in on the saloon stories. "My grandmother is a cook. A very good cook."

Billy grinned. "I love to eat. What kind of stuff does she make?"

"Well." Colleen studied Billy. "She cooks for the men who come to the saloon." When he kept his smile, she added, "We all live in some rooms above the saloon. Ma cooks meals for the customers."

Billy nodded. "How many men does she cook for?"

Colleen shrugged. "Fifty maybe."

"How much flour do you figure she runs through a week?"

Colleen smiled. "I'm not sure. A lot."

Billy put his hands in his back pockets and tapped his foot as the music started. "My uncle runs the saloon here, but he has to cook for himself. Only knows how to make hash, so nobody asks him to bother."

"Well, hey, Billy. Where is Colleen?" Wade was wearing a red necktie and had his hair slicked back. He nodded at Colleen, but didn't speak to her.

"Here I am." Laura hurried across the floor. Even without the fancy braids and bonnet, she looked beautiful.

As the music continued to play, more and more students from the spelling bee moved into the room. Nobody danced. By the fifth song, the only people out on the floor were the Eastons and two elderly ladies who were in charge of the punch and cookies.

"Should we dance?" asked Wade. "This party only lasts for an hour."

Billy laughed. "Took me longer than that to wash up."

Laura looked at Colleen. "Do you want to?"

"I meant, do *you* want to dance with *me*," said Wade. He took Laura's hand and pulled her toward the dance floor.

"I have a headache," Laura blurted out.

"Me, too," said Colleen.

"What?" Wade looked displeased.

"Well, you can't control the weather, and you can't control a headache," Billy said good-naturedly. "Why don't you go rest a spell, ladies, and I'll catch up with you later."

Billy stuck his hat back on his head and smiled as he walked across the floor.

"Good night," Colleen said shortly. She walked until she was out in the lobby. She glanced at the grandfather clock, wishing the hands would fly around so it could be morning.

Colleen slid into a leather chair, listening to the music. Suddenly, she sat up straight. The candy. She had completely forgotten to get Brian his present! She hurried over to the front desk. Nobody was behind the desk, so she tapped the bell.

"Coming!" Mr. Loomis came out from a back room, wiping his mouth with a napkin.

"Mr. Loomis, could you tell me where I could get some candy? I need it to take on the stage."

Mr. Loomis looked up at the clock. "Pretty late to be thinking about candy, Miss. Might have to wait till morning. Your stage won't be leaving till ten or so. Best bet is to run across the street in the morning and get it."

"Where across the street? By the barber shop?"

"No, little bit farther down. Right next to where you got on the wagon to head on out to the school," explained Mr. Loomis. "You can't miss it once you get outside."

"Thanks." Colleen walked slowly to the narrow front windows and tried to peer out down the street. She would have to wake up early so she would have time to get the candy. Colleen looked over to the dining room entrance. Laura wasn't much of a friend. She hadn't even bothered to come out and see if Colleen was okay. Well, phooey on her.

Colleen went to the front door and opened it. She would just step outside a second to make sure she could see the store. Tomorrow she would get plenty of candy for Brian and Becky.

As soon as she stepped outside, Colleen heard a scream, followed by a man's deep laughter.

23

Colleen reached for the doorknob. She should run and get Mr. Easton. Someone was in trouble!

"Wade, stop it. You're gonna fall! I swear, you're the silliest boy I've ever met."

"Fear not, lovely lady. I am a trained professional."

"Wade, I mean it."

Colleen heard more laughter. She took a step closer to the porch swing. It sounded like Laura and Wade.

"Now, if I can walk this rail, you gotta go back inside and dance with me," cried Wade. "Promise?"

"I'll dance with you, just get down. You're making me nervous! Boys in Colorado Springs aren't nearly so brave!"

Colleen tiptoed closer and peered around the side of the hotel. Laura sounded more excited than scared.

"Here goes!"

Colleen held her breath as Wade started out across a shaky tightrope he had made by placing a rail between two windows. He was several feet over Laura's head.

"Get down, Wade!" Laura cried. "You're gonna crack your head open."

"Well, from what you say, you're just the lady to sew me up. I ain't never dated a doctor's gal before."

Wade's arms flapped up and down as he skillfully walked across the rail. Colleen frowned. Wade knew what he was doing. He probably showed this trick off to every new girl in town.

"Very nice, now get down!" Laura laughed.

Wade turned to make a small bow. He jerked forward, then, as he tried to straighten up, flopped backwards, landing on a pile of loose lumber.

"Oh, my arm!" hollered Wade. "My arm!"

Laura screamed and raced to Wade's side. "Are you okay?"

"Pop my arm back in!" cried Wade. He tried to scoot forward, then grabbed his left shoulder. "Hurry, Colleen. Pa said he'd kill me if I tried walking the rail again. Hurry, pop it back quick!"

Laura stood up and ran her fingers through her hair again and again. "Pop what where? Wade, what are you talking about? What's wrong with your arm?"

Sweat dotted Wade's forehead. "I dislocated my shoulder. Happened before. Shove it back in." Wade wiped his forehead. "This hurts, Colleen. Hurry up! You know what to do, do it!"

"But I don't know how to pop an arm!" cried Laura.

"You told me last night you popped the Reverend's when he fell off the pulpit! Said you popped Richard's, too."

Laura took a step forward, then three back. "But that was a couple of weeks ago. I forget what I did. I better go get help. I think people in Weisport treat this ailment differently."

"You crazy? Now get back here!" Wade sounded angry. "Pa's gonna break both my arms if he finds me here."

Laura burst into tears. "I don't know how. I'll end up making it worse."

"Just *do* it!" Wade leaned back against the boards and groaned.

Colleen slid both feet over the railing and hopped down, hurrying down the alley.

"I'll go get help," cried Laura. When she turned, she saw Colleen and raced into her arms. "Oh, Colleen! Help Wade! Do you know how to pop an arm?"

Colleen knelt down beside Wade. She reached for his arm, but he jerked away. "Get away from me, Laura."

"I know what I'm doing," Colleen said. She tried

to keep her voice calm. "Do you want me to try and help or not?"

"No!" Wade pushed Colleen aside and reached for Laura. "Colleen, please, I'm beggin' you. This really hurts."

Laura knelt down beside Wade, pulling Colleen closer. "I don't know a thing about popping arms. This is the real Colleen. Her ma is Dr. Quinn. Colleen knows how to help. I don't. I . . ." Laura scrambled to her feet. Two large tears streamed down her cheeks. "I . . . I don't know a *thing* anymore."

Wade sat up, holding his arm, glaring at both girls. "What's going on here? How many Colleens are there?"

"Just one." Colleen reached out and gently lifted Wade's elbow. "Does this hurt?"

"Course it hurts," snapped Wade. "Are you girls playing some mean trick on me?" He pushed Colleen's hand away. "I don't want you twisting my arm off like some overcooked chicken wing."

"Do you want me to fix your arm or not?" Colleen stood up. "Let's get his pa. He can ask Dr. Demos to come over."

"No!" Wade sat up. "Dr. Demos told me next time I dislocated this arm from being stupid, he was gonna sew it to my side till I got some sense."

"Which might be never," Colleen said.

"So, whichever one of you girls is the daughter of Dr. Quinn, go do your stuff," said Wade.

He closed his eyes. "I just hope you know what you're doing."

"You can at least say please," snapped Laura. "Colleen doesn't have to lift a finger to help you, Mr. Smart Aleck."

Colleen tried not to smile at Laura.

"Please," said Wade quietly.

Colleen knelt down, taking Wade's arm in her own and gently moving it back and forth. "Hold tight, now," she said. Laura knelt down and grabbed Wade's hand as Colleen expertly popped his shoulder back into the socket.

"Wow!" said Laura. "You're good, Colleen."

"She's . . ." Wade bit his lip and sighed. "Thanks."

"I guess you don't feel much like dancing, do you, Wade?" asked Laura. She looked up at Colleen and grinned.

Wade struggled to his feet, ignoring Colleen's and Laura's outstretched hands. "If you two were the last girls in the state of Colorado, I wouldn't ask either one of you to dance."

Colleen nodded. "I guess we had that coming. We didn't mean any harm."

"It was just an experiment," added Laura.

Wade grabbed his arm and walked past them. "Well, next time, I pray I won't be the fella in on the experiment."

"Hey!"

Everyone turned and watched as Lorraine

stomped down the alley. "You guys missed me getting the trophy."

"Sorry," said Colleen. "We were . . . " Colleen stopped. She didn't want to tell another lie, no matter how small. Her ma always told her that the truth, no matter how bad, was still a whole sight better than a dirty lie.

"I hurt my shoulder," Wade said. He brushed past Colleen and Laura, not looking at either one. "I didn't see something."

"Well, can't that happen to us all?" said Lorraine. She slapped Wade on his back. Wade winced, but kept walking. "Come on inside and let me tell you about the time my uncle walked right into a puddle of quicksand. Never saw it till he was screaming for help!"

Wade glared at Colleen and Laura as he walked by. "Must have been in Colorado Springs."

When Lorraine and Wade rounded the corner, Laura covered her face with both hands.

"Don't start crying on me," said Colleen. "We made a mistake, but Wade deserved what he got. He can't treat people like that."

Laura's shoulders shook.

"Laura, it was mostly my fault. I didn't *have* to trade places with you."

Laura dropped her hands and laughed out loud. "He was such a fake. Worse than we were, Colleen. And he can't even switch back."

Colleen grinned. "I know. Maybe he'll rethink things. Like us."

Both girls were quiet as they walked back up onto the hotel porch.

Laura sank onto a bench and sighed. "Well, I guess we'll be going back to Colorado Springs empty-handed."

"What do you mean?" Colleen sat down beside Laura.

"No trophy."

Colleen smiled. "Reverend won't care. We tried. Besides, I don't think we're going home empty-handed at all." Colleen stood up and took Laura's hand. "See anybody empty-handed around here?"

Laura started to laugh. "No."

As the two girls walked back inside hand in hand, the fiddle music became livelier. Colleen knew Lorraine had to be the one playing, or maybe it was just her own heart. A heart busy beating out how wonderful it felt to have a new friend.

About the Author

Colleen O'Shaughnessy McKenna began writing as a child, when she sent off a script for the *Bonanza* series. Ms. McKenna is best known for her Murphy books, the inspiration for which comes from her own family.

In addition to the eight books in the Murphy series, Ms. McKenna has written *Merry Christmas, Miss McConnell!*, the young adult novel *The Brightest Light*, and *Good Grief . . . Third Grade*, a spin-off of the Murphy series. Ms. McKenna is also the author of a second book based on the characters from *Dr. Quinn, Medicine Woman*.

A former elementary school teacher, Ms. McKenna lives in Pittsburgh, Pennsylvania, with her husband and four children.